The Fifth Di...
April 2024

Features

54	*The Uber Cat and Dragon Owner Manual* Reviewed by Lisa Timpf
56	*Prey* Reviewed by Lee Clark Zumpe
75	Who's Who

Short Stories

11	Flame by Maureen Bowden
22	A Nascent Rose by Lawrence Buentello
68	Knowing Then What I Know Now by Christian Riley

Flash Fiction

43	Mechanical Mannequins by Priya Sridhar
60	Context by Gustavo Bondoni
65	The Tenth Symphony by Matias Travieso-Diaz

Poetry

42	Sometime After the Apocalypse: Family Loyalty, Part 1 by Terrie Leigh Relf
51	The Beasts of Night by Sandy DeLuca

Illustrations

50	Sorrow by Sandy DeLuca

THE STAFF OF THE FIFTH DI...:

EDITOR: Tyree Campbell
WEBMASTER: H David Blalock
COVER DESIGNERS: Laura Givens; Marcia A. Borell

Cover art "Professor" by Paula Hammond
Cover design by Laura Givens

Vol. V, No.1   April 2024

The Fifth Di... is published three times a year on the 1st day of April, August, and December in the United States of America by Hiraeth Publishing, P.O. Box 1248, Tularosa, NM, 88352. Copyright 2024 by Hiraeth Publishing. All rights revert to authors and artists upon publication except as noted in selected individual contracts. Nothing may be reproduced in whole or in part without written permission from the authors and artists. Any similarity between places and persons mentioned in the fiction or semi-fiction and real places or persons living or dead is coincidental. Writers and artists guidelines are available online at www.hiraethsffh.com. Guidelines are also available upon request from Hiraeth Publishing, P.O. Box 1248, Tularosa, NM, 88352, if request is accompanied by a self-addressed #10 envelope with a first-class US stamp. Editor: Tyree Campbell.

A Little Help, Please

In the world of the small indie press we fight a never-ending battle for attention to our work, as writers and in publishing. Here's an example: big publishers [you know who they are] have gobs of $$$ that they can devote to advertising and marketing. Here at Hiraeth Publishing, our advertising budget consists of the deposits for whatever soda bottles and aluminum cans we can find alongside the highways. Anti-littering laws make our task even more difficult . . . ☺

That's where YOU come in. YOU are our best promoter. YOU are the one who can tell others about us. Just send 'em to our website, tell them about our store. That's all. Just that.

Of course, we don't mind if you talk us up. We're pretty good, you know. We have some award-winning and award-nominated writers and artists, plus other voices well-deserving to be heard [not everyone wins awards, right?] but our publications are read-worthy nevertheless.

That number once again is:
www.hiraethsffh.com

Friend us on Facebook at Hiraeth Publishing
Follow us on Twitter at @HiraethPublish1

Pevely Keiser in:
THE IPHAJEAN LARK

Five hundred years into the future, Pevely Keiser is the capo of the criminal organization called Temmen. Temmen runs itself, for the most part, with only a few nudges from Pevely to keep people in line. Lately she has two things on her mind. She wants to do something good and useful with the funds that accrue to the gang. And she wants a companion or two to help her…and perhaps to share her bed, for she well knows it's lonely at the top.

In the process of training her two new assistants (and possible companions) Pevely comes across a young woman being chased. Taking her on board, Pevely soon learns of a devastating conspiracy that threatens the Confederation with totalitarian rule. The key to the solution lies in the hands of one of her employees, but is it the right key? Only the corporate hierarch who leads the conspiracy knows for sure. And he is the father of the woman Pevely rescued.

https://www.hiraethsffh.com/product-page/iphajean-lark-by-tyree-campbell

New from Hiraeth Publishing!!
The Spark
By Stephen C. Curro

Katrina grew up in a frigid world ruled by a tyrant. By day, she works as a mechanic. At night, she becomes the Ace, the King's personal assassin. She's not proud of her job, but she's accepted that it's the way things are. At least she has her boyfriend Dez and his little brother Uriah to light her life.

When Katrina is ordered to quash a rebel attack on the King's Command Center, she thinks it's just another job. But as she uncovers the plot, she is shocked to learn that Dez may be involved with the dissidents. Now Katrina must make an impossible choose—eliminate the one she loves, or defy the King she swore to serve.

The Spark is a sci-fi thriller about love, betrayal, and how the futures of others, even a whole civilization, can be determined through a single choice.

https://www.hiraethsffh.com/product-page/the-spark-by-stephen-c-curro

The Oculist's Daughter
By Angel Favazza

The Oculist's Daughter by Angel Favazza is a steampunker in the old west. It's got a semi-mad scientist (her dad), her, of course, plus outlaws, Indians, Wyoming, a poison gas for killing natives, and an Indian guide. It all adds up to a rollicking adventure.

https://www.hiraethsffh.com/product-page/oculist-s-daughter-by-angel-favazza

Living Bad Dreams
By Denise Hatfield

When dreams come alive, there's no telling where they will lead. Everything changes when you realize that, dream or no dream, you're going to die. What do you do then?

Type: Novella
Audience: adults
Ordering Link:
Print Edition ($9.00):
https://www.hiraethsffh.com/product-page/living-bad-dreams-by-denise-hatfield-1

ePub edition ($2.99):
https://www.hiraethsffh.com/product-page/living-bad-dreams-by-denise-hatfield-2

Feed Me Wicked Things
By Lee Clark Zumpe

There is tremendous power in words, and few writers can draw upon that power better than Lee Clark Zumpe. In "Feed Me Wicked Things" he summons topics ranging from the poignant horror of Srebrenica in the 1990s to the lynching trees of the 1890s, from the futility of assassination to the thoughts of a lonely passing. Evocative and provocative, Zumpe once read cannot be forgotten.

https://www.hiraethsffh.com/product-page/feed-me-wicked-things-by-lee-clark-zumpe

Flame
Maureen Bowden

"I never see thy face but I think upon hellfire"
William Shakespeare; Henry IV part 1, Act 3, scene 3

My name is Jessica Bailey. My father, Robert, is human. My mother is not. I'd learned to live with the situation but never found the opportunity to turn it to my advantage, until a dodgy millionaire business entrepreneur threatened the wellbeing of my ten-year old half-brother Oscar, known as Ozzie.

My father's wife Emma rang me in a state of agitation, not unusual for her. She's human, daft as a brush but good hearted. "Jess, something terrible has happened. That grubby money-grabber, Bernie Morgan, has bought the kids' football pitch and he's going to build a casino on it, with one-arm bandits, roulette tables, the whole razzmatazz. We're having a protest march on Saturday. Are you in?"

"Slow down, Emz," I said. "He can't do that. The Council would never give him planning permission."

"He's got it. Probably lined a few pockets or threatened to expose a dirty secret or two. It's the headline in 'The Orifice.' Bring your student friends along. They enjoy a good protest, especially that mad girl, Sophie Melancamp."

Our local rag, 'The Daily Oracle,' commonly known as the 'The Orifice,' seldom let truth, overwhelming evidence or the laws of physics get in way of a good headline, but Bent Bernie had a reputation for getting his own way, so I gave the story some credence. I turned up for the protest march on Saturday morning, accompanied by Sophie and Wei Yen, who shared my student accommodation on Riverside University campus. The town folk joined us in their hundreds. Many had children who were members of 'Riverside Junior Giants FC.' Sophie was wielding a banner emblazoned with the threat, 'Bog Off, Bernie, Or Else…' The painted words were surrounded by realistic red and orange flames. She positioned herself at the front and led us like Boudicca in Lycra leggings. 'The Orifice' sent along its roving reporter, lone paparazza and general dirt-digger, Julie Gahooly to immortalise events, and we set off in high spirits, encouraged by cheers and whoops from onlookers, all the way to the Mayor's house.

Bernie had friends in high places so the police retaliated. We were met with truncheons and tear gas canisters. The peaceful march degenerated into a riot. Dozens ended up in Riverside hospital's over-crowded A & E department and Sophie Melancamp was arrested for allegedly inappropriately touching a police officer. In her defence she claimed. "He stuck his hand inside my bra so I grabbed anything I could reach. It was tit for tat, innit?"

She was released and charges against her were dropped on condition that she agreed not to post her version of the incident on Facebook. Sophie did, however, have the last laugh. Julie Gahooly had the police officer's exploration on film and it made the front page of the Saturday evening edition of 'The Orifice.'

I couldn't sleep on Saturday night. The image of the flames on Sophie's banner kept nagging at me. Finally, I realised what my subconscious mind was suggesting. It was something I should have done long ago, but first I needed to talk it through with someone who would understand. The only two candidates were my father and Emma. It had to be her. I knew Dad would find the prospect too difficult to confront. I wanted to contact my mother.

* * *

The memory of my seventh birthday party flooded back to me. My friends sang 'Happy Birthday' and as I took a breath, preparing to blow out the candles on my cake, I glanced at Dad. He was staring at the flickering flames. There were tears in his eyes.

After my friends left, with goodie bags and slices of cake, I said. "What's wrong, Daddy? You look sad."

He sat me on his lap. "You're a big girl now, Jess. It's time I told you about your mother."

"You already told me. She died when I was born."

He shook his head. "I told you that when you were too young to understand what she really is."

His words unsettled me and I shivered. "Will I be frightened?"

He smiled. "No, Jess. It's a wonderful story. Listen. Four and a half billion years ago the earth was a ball of fire. There was a living being on the earth even then. It was your mother. In time the earth cooled, but she still lives wherever there's even a single flame. She asked me to tell you about her when you reached your seventh birthday. She said if you ever need her, find a flame and call her."

"What will she look like?"

"She can take any form she chooses. When we were together she was a beautiful lady. That's probably how she'll show herself to you."

"But what is she and what's her name?"

"She's the Essence of Fire. I called her Flame."

* * *

Thirteen years had passed since then and I'd never contacted her. Now it was time. I rang Emma on Sunday morning. "Hi, Emz. Can you get a couple of hours off work tomorrow? Fake a migraine or something. I need to talk to you while Dad's at work. Don't tell him."

"What's up, Jess?" She said. "Are you in some sort of trouble?"

"No, I'm fine. I have an idea of how to save the footie club. Dad might not like it but I think it's our best option."

'Okay. You're not making much sense but I'll listen. Come over after nine o'clock. Ozzie will be in school then."

At half past nine we were sitting in Emma's tidy, tastefully furnished living room, a refreshing change from the cluttered chaos of my student flat. She poured me a coffee. "I'm waiting," she said. "Let's hear it."

"I'm going to contact Flame."

"What? You can't. She's dangerous."

"That's why we need her on our side. Bent Bernie has powerful friends but they won't be able to protect him from her."

She groaned. "Who's going to protect us from her? She burns things. Robert still has scorch marks on-"

"Spare me the nitty-gritty, Emz."

She blushed. "Sorry, I tend to forget that he's your dad." As I said: daft as a brush.

"He coped and so will we. She's my mother and it's time I got to know her." I gulped down my coffee, ran into the kitchen and took the matches off the shelf on which they were stored, too high for Ozzie to reach. I took them back into the living room. "I'd like you here with me, but if you don't feel safe I'll understand if you'd rather go upstairs."

"Not likely. Just hang on." She fled, returning a few minutes later carrying a large jug of water and a blanket. She placed the jug on the coffee table and draped the blanket over the couch, covering the seat and scatter cushions. "I want to make sure she doesn't set fire to my soft furnishings. Be careful with the match. Blow it out before it burns your fingers and put it back in the matchbox."

"Don't fuss. I'm a big girl now." I struck the match. It flared and I called, "Flame!" A column of fire appeared, swirling and swaying until taking the shape of a slender young woman. Her wild, curly red hair reached to her waist. She wore tight black leather trousers and a black tee-shirt emblazoned with red lettering spelling out 'Don't Play With Fire.' She was beautiful.

I said, "Hello, Mother."

She said, "Hello, Jessica. Good to meet you at last. You certainly took your time." She turned to Emma. "You must be Robert's woman. How is he?"

Emma glanced at the water jug then back to Flame. "Very well, thank you, and my name's Emma. How are you?"

"Curious. You ladies must have had a reason to summon me. May I sit?" She lowered her leather-clad backside onto the couch. We smelled burning. She leapt up again, narrowly missing being soaked as Emma hurled water over the smouldering blanket.

We removed it and checked that the couch was intact. "Sorry, about that." Flame said. "These things happen when you're dealing with the Essence of Fire. It's the nature of the beast, innit?"

The slang grated on my ears, "Don't say, innit," I said. "It makes you sound uneducated." Ridiculous thing to say, I know, but I was in a state of some confusion.

"I'll bear that in mind. I was trying to sound human. Don't your friends speak like that?"

I thought of Sophie Melancamp. "One of them does, but she does a lot of things I wouldn't expect you to do."

"However, there is clearly something you do expect me to do. I'll sit while you explain. I believe I've cooled down now." She sat before we could answer.

We explained about Bernie Morgan's take-over and plans for the football pitch. "Children need fresh air and exercise," Emma said. "We don't want them to spend all their leisure time playing games on their tablets, talking to each other on their phones, and risking being targeted by some of the monsters on the internet."

"It's not just the boys who'll be missing out," I said. "The girls' team won the junior league cup last year."

Flame smiled. "And we must support the sisterhood, must we not? I'm in, ladies. We need to plan our campaign, but first, tell me about yourself, Jessica. What are you doing with your life?"

I sat beside her. "Call me Jess. I'm at University."

"Do you live with Robert and Emma?"

"No. I share a flat with two friends."

"What are you all studying?"

"I'm not sure about Sophie. I've never seen her study anything and she doesn't go to lectures," an image of the banner blazed into my mind, "but, she's very good at art. Wei Yen and I are studying astrophysics. She's the clever one. It bewilders me. Maybe you could help me make sense of it."

She patted my hand. "I expect I could, but humans are not yet ready to ask the right questions. Now, let's plan our campaign. When is this spec of cosmic grit intending to commence building his pleasure dome?"

Emma said, "They're going to start digging up the pitch next week so they can lay the foundations."

Flame smiled. "Using the science of mechanics, no doubt. Where there's electricity there's a spark, where there's fuel there's fire, and internal combustion engines are fun. I love combustion. It tickles." She stopped smiling. "I'll burn them."

I said, "Please don't kill or injure anyone, Mother. We don't want that on our conscience."

"I promise. No flesh shall burn. I need to know the location at which the machines are held, and the addresses of all the employees. I'll burn all their vehicles to hinder their activities as much as possible."

Emma said, "We could find out from 'The Orifice.' They have spies everywhere."

Flame frowned. "Of whose orifice are we speaking?"

I said, "Sorry, nobody's orifice. It's what we call our local newspaper." I turned to Emma, "Sophie's bezzy mates with Julie Gahooly these days. She'll get her to deliver the goodies in exchange for a good story."

Flame said, "When you have the goodies strike a match and I'll be there." She vanished.

That evening I told Sophie that Emma and I knew someone who could swat Bent Bernie flat, and I explained what we needed. "Can you get the information from Julie Gahooly with no questions asked? There'll be a story in it for her."

Sophie whooped. "No problem. Offer JG a story and she'll bring you the head of a saint on a platter."

JG delivered the goodies. The following evening, Sophie, Wei Yen and I sat on our battered, moth-eaten sofa and examined the list she'd sent by phone. I'd have to call Flame so we could show it to her. What would she think of the dump I called home? The coffee table was littered with magazines, Wei Yen's books and study notes, a broken laptop, remnants of last Christmas's home-made paper garlands, a half-eaten take-away pizza and a sock. The wall behind the couch was partially covered by an abstract mural Sophie had left unfinished when she ran out of paint. It's anyone's guess what it was supposed to be and she said she couldn't remember. A Wooden Buddha with one ear missing, as a result of one of Sophie's parties getting out of control, stood in the alcove at the side of the chimney breast and surveyed the décor with his enigmatic smile, oozing inner serenity. I hoped my mother wasn't house-proud.

Sophie said, "What happens now?"

"Something really weird," I said. Don't freak out."

Wei Yen said, "Do you need me? The only weirdness I'm interested in is black holes and I have studying to do."

"That's okay," I said. "We won't disturb you."

"Thanks. Good luck with your freakery." She grabbed her dog-eared copy of Stephen Hawking's 'Brief Answers to the Big Questions,' and retreated to her bedroom.

Sophie said, "I don't know why she bothers. The universe is what it is."

I said, "She wants to observe it."

"Why? Observing it won't change it."

"It might. It changes people. When anyone looks at you I've noticed you do that pouty thing with your mouth."

She laughed. "Are you saying the universe pouts if we look at it?"

I shrugged, "Dunno. Ask Wei Yen."

"I'd rather not know, thanks. Let's get on with the weirdness. What do we do?"

"You do nothing except fill a jug of water and hang onto it just in case."

"Of what?"

"Of anything catching fire."

She found a dusty jug under the kitchen sink and filled it from the tap. "This doesn't have anything to do with astrophysics, does it?"

"Possibly, but don't worry about it." I struck a match and Flame appeared before I had time to call her name. I said, "Sophie, meet my mother."

Sophie's mouth fell open. Regaining her composure, she said "Cool."

Flame said, "Not yet, my dear, but I won't sit until I am, so you can put down your water vessel."

Sophie glanced at me. I nodded. She pushed the sock off the coffee table to make room for the jug.

Flame said, "I'm cool now." Avoiding a broken spring she sat on the sofa.

Sophie sat beside her and showed her JG's list. "Will you be able to remember all that?"

"My dear girl, I remember everything I've seen, heard, thought and felt for the last four and a half billion years. Your list of goodies is what you would call a doddle. Leave it with me. I'll be observing how the situation develops, and when the children regain possession of their pitch I'll be there to cheer them on. I've never been to a football match. I look forward to the experience. See you there, girls." She glanced at the one-eared Buddha, "I met that gentleman in the flesh."

"Is there much resemblance?" I said.

"No. He had two ears and he was better looking." She blew me a kiss and then she vanished.

On the morning that the digging was scheduled to start, the protesters gathered at the football pitch. Sophie brought her banner and wore a very short skirt, Emma wore the 'Junior Giants FC' strip, and Wei Yen wore a tee shirt adorned with a painting of an abandoned wheelchair and a human figure walking into a starry sky.

We spotted Julie Gahooly with her camera slung across her shoulder. Sophie waved to her, "Hi, JG."

The lone paparazza joined us, flashing her dental implants, "Hi, girls." She glanced at Wei Yen. "Love the tee-shirt. Who is he?"

Wei Yen said, "A friend. His name's Stephen."

Julie turned to Sophie. "Introduce me to your fellow conspirators, Sophe."

Sophie said, "Jess, Emz, Wei Yen. You all know JG, of course."

We exchanged nods.

Julie said, "Have you heard about the fires?"

Sophie said. "What fires? Spill."

She spilled. "At about three o'clock this morning all 'Morgan Constructions PLC' equipment caught fire, as well as every car owned by the proprietor and his employees. Apparently the fuel tanks exploded. By the time the fire engines arrived all they found was burned-out heaps of twisted metal." She winked at Sophie. "Don't worry, I won't be telling anyone about the small favour I did for you, Sophe. I'll be discretion personified."

First time for everything.

She continued. "I've got another great story for tonight's edition. I had a phone call about an hour ago from Madame Jaquetta, the clairvoyant who writes our horoscope column. She said a fiery angel appeared to her and told her Bent Bernie's plan for the casino was cursed because the spirits of every late great football legend were guarding the children's pitch and they were having none of it, so Bernie had better take his dodgy enterprises to the other end of the country and never come back."

Emma said, "Madame Jaquetta gets my horoscope wrong every time. I think she's a fake."

Julie said, "She is, but she believes in the fiery angel. Personally, I think it was more likely to be the Essence of Fire."

My head spun. "How did you know about...?"

She laughed. "I've been doing this job a long time, Jess. I've learned a lot and seen a lot of strange things."

Wei Yen said. "Like what?"

"Like ghosts, demons, shape-shifters. I was bitten by a vampire once. He was a dish."

Emma said. "I've heard they usually are. He didn't turn you into a vamp, though?"

"No, but he gave me a humdinger of a hickie. I had to wear my Burberry scarf for a month."

An hour passed and it became clear that there'd be no digging today. The protesters made their way home.

The Monday edition of 'The Orifice' carried the story that 'Morgan Constructions PLC' had closed down, and a widespread rumour claimed that Madame Jaquetta's fiery angel had appeared to Bernie, repeating the warning on Sophie's banner: "Bog Off Bernie Or Else..." The Town Council had reclaimed the football pitch by compulsory purchase and in a magnanimous gesture had gifted it to 'Riverside Junior Giants FC.' With ownership of its own pitch the future of the club was secured. The by-line of the story indicated that it was written by Julie Gahooly. No surprise there.

The club organised a celebratory match between two mixed teams of boys and girls. Ozzie was in one of them. I asked Emma. "Will Dad come to watch him play?"

She shook her head. "I hope you don't mind, Jess, but I felt I had to tell him that you'd contacted Flame and she'd be with us at the match. He was pleased. He wants you to get to know each other but he doesn't want to see her so he's keeping away." She squeezed my hand. "You must understand. He said he wants to keep her in his past where she belongs, and I told him he was right." She's not as daft as I thought.

The mixed teams were a joy to behold. The crowd cheered both sides and nobody cared who won. It ended in a draw: the perfect result. After the final whistle the spectators invaded the pitch with crates of soft drinks from a couple of major supermarkets and fresh-made cakes from a local bakery. We had a party. JG's camera flashed along with her dental implants. I spotted my mother deep in conversation with Wei Yen and I felt a pang of jealousy. Does she think I'm not intelligent enough for serious discussion? Maybe I should show more interest in black holes.

She left Wei Yen's side and joined me. "I'll be leaving soon, Jess, but I hope it won't be another thirteen years before you call me again."

All the puzzlement and sadness I'd felt while growing up without her erupted in anger. "If you're so concerned why did you leave Dad and me when I was born?"

She led me away from the party to a bench in the park alongside the football pitch and we sat together. "Tell, me Jess," she said, "Do you enjoy swimming?"

"Yes, very much. What does that have to do with anything?"

"If you like it so much why don't you live in the sea?"

I began to understand. "It's not my element. I couldn't survive in it."

She nodded. "Of course you couldn't, just as I can't survive for more than a year or so in this element. I had to leave you and return to the element of fire."

"So why did you have a child with a human? It was a stupid thing to do."

She nodded. "I agree, but Robert and I were in love, and love often leads people to do stupid things. You may have noticed."

I smiled. "Point taken."

"I hope I'm forgiven because there's something I need you to understand. I'm immortal and humans are not, but you have a dual genetic heritage. The day will come when your human life ends. If you wish, you can then join me as the Essence of Fire, and the multi-verse will be ours to explore together."

The prospect terrified me and I shoved it to back of my mind to contemplate later. Much later. "I'll consider it, but right now I'd be happy for us to just get to know each other better."

"Whatever you say, Jess. Just strike a match and I'll be there."

Something was nagging at me. "One more thing: what were you and Wei Yen talking about earlier?"

"Astrophysics."

"What about it, them, whatever?"

"Ah, that's beyond your understanding right now, but in time I believe Wei Yen may be the one to ask the right questions. Now, give me a hug before I go. I won't scorch you. I'm cool."

I hugged her. "You certainly are."

Whispers of Magic
By Maureen Bowden

Legends and unusual characters abound in England, where you never know who or what you might meet in the forests. Maureen Bowden introduces you to them in these stories of magic and misdirection…and invites you to stay.

Maureen Bowden is a Liverpudlian, living with her musician husband in North Wales. In addition to stories, she also writes song lyrics, mostly comic political satire, set to traditional melodies. She loves her family and friends, rock 'n' roll, Shakespeare, and cats.

https://www.hiraethsffh.com/product-page/whispers-of-magic

A Nascent Rose
Lawrence Buentello

Day 150

I don't know why I keep expecting *Dinosauria* DNA to differ significantly from DNA sequencing of my time. Perhaps it's an elitist tendency.

The species of *Albertonykus borealis* I sequenced today, its small size allowing me to eschew euthanasia, bore many similarities to avian sequences from my time. Perhaps I've been expecting a fantastic representation of ancient life rather than inevitable close similarities, despite my temporal displacement. The meter-long specimen I processed, pale yellow and slightly mottled like a fish of the coral reef, gazed at me inquisitively through apricot-colored eyes before I released it into the forest, its long, feathered tail whipping in the air as if it were celebrating its freedom. It vanished into the undergrowth, suddenly camouflaged by the yellow-green flora.

I find myself increasingly anthropomorphizing my specimens as time goes on; I wonder if this symptom will lead to worse mental aberrations.

I didn't realize my work would progress so quickly. Perhaps I thought it would be a life's endeavor, but, of course, I'm using limited resources. I only have two more pods to fill. And then—

In my undergraduate days, I spent my spare time phasing paleontology references, works on paleobotany, historical geology; my primary phasing on physics and biology should have primed my neural loading to capacity, but I grew fascinated by studies of the past. I didn't know then I was destined to become part of the literature.

I'm not an isolationist by choice, but by nature, so I suppose it's no great sacrifice. No undergraduate will phase the name 'Morrisey' in those references, though I may be written of eventually, as a dazzling success or a pathetic footnote of history. I suspect the latter.

Proving temporal replacement could be accomplished didn't manifest as the most difficult part of our project— justifying the commitment of so many resources and such a high expenditure of energy proved a near impossibility, and, according to moral purists, reasonable human beings shouldn't commit suicide, which the project essentially demanded. Perhaps that's why we've had so few examples of historical anomalies. No one really knows the effect one hundred million, or five hundred million years will produce to dissolve even the most durable technology, but I suspect it will perform an admirable job. I hope they find the pods; but I'll never know. None were found before I left, though the project had lain in drafting modules for years.

I'll have to devise a purpose for my life once our profoundly finite goal is accomplished. But what?

First things first—I have to finish filling the pods.

Then I'll consider my future, as humorous as that sounds. I always have the needle if life proves unlivable, but I'd rather conjure new pursuits before resorting to self-destruction. I am, after all, the solitary type.

Day 155

The plants, the insects, the fungi, the spores—I don't mind killing these things to acquire their genetic material, I've done so a thousand times in the laboratory in the past. But killing animals in *this* environment disturbs me. I've located dead specimens, but the difficulty in indentifying carcasses requires me to know exactly what DNA I'm extruding. As I reported earlier, I experimented with a 'capture and release' approach, but lost too many larger specimens to justify the practice. I think I've killed over a hundred animals by now, released just as many back into their environments, non-sentient organisms to be certain, but the number of animals I've destroyed still disturbs me. Sedation is not an option: what pharmaceutical drug properly anesthetizes a sauropod? Would the same drug have the same effect on an ornithopod? A carnosaur? And where would I find local ingredients for these drugs?

I feel as if I'm on an alien planet, moving through flora and fauna deserving my respect, but these organisms have been dead for nearly a hundred million years. Why should I care?

Filling the first pod had been fairly time consuming (see my summation for Day 30). Though the computer coded the diamond lattice layers with the specifics of the genetic material, I brooded long hours over the general descriptions of the subjects. Then the realization came to me that minute specifications were pointless—the genetic mapping would render a facsimile perfectly, so I only needed to provide a general description and let future generations worry over the binomial nomenclature. Cladistics will seem like primitive methodology. The rest were filled at an exponential rate as my skills increased. Perhaps I should have been more judicious, but the project would be significantly damaged if I died tomorrow. I could fall off a ledge, or some predator could take advantage of a security-fail, and then what?

But I'm trying to be more discerning with the final pods. Only large specimens for the time being. If I find something extraordinary, some unknown plants of fascinating dimensions, I might include those as well. The problem is—we just didn't *know*—

In this environment, a thousand creatures exist of which we knew nothing from the fossil record, animals that left no fossils, or whose fossils weren't discovered by my time. And they're *beautiful*, exotic, tantalizing examples of evolution. If the Temporal Commission finds the pods where I've buried them, in the area our computer models calculated as the badlands of North America, at least one of them, then they'll know, too. They might read these words describing the beauty of a world they never knew, of the variety, of the splendor of the world as it was and will never be again, unless they successfully regenerate these plants and animals through the records I've left for cloning labs.

I've come to believe the gulf between my understanding of this prehistoric world, as chronicled by academic reconstructions of a dead ecosystem, and the living reality all around me has affected my sense of myself—no imaginary bestiary could have prepared me for the actual sight of these incredible animals moving through their forests, jungles, and wastelands. Saurians, pterosaurs, ancestral birds, early mammals all live together in a pristine world fully green with exotic plants and trees, floral species long extinct in my time towering into the sky. These are living creatures, replete with vivid coloration, bright feathers, iridescent flesh, and anatomical variations never before seen by human eyes. When

I first witnessed a pair of smaller tyrannosaurs in the wild, marking territory amongst the trees, their dun and purple dermis gleaming in the morning sunlight, their bright eyes studying the tree line for prey, I couldn't convince myself of their reality.

An esthetic exists in this world that can't be recorded mathematically, it simply has to be experienced.

It is the Earth, and yet it *isn't* the Earth; it is so magnificently *something else* that no words can illustrate it. I wake in the morning to a sunrise that is just as bright as any I knew as a child, but the sky isn't as blue, the clouds are more translucent, the storms are much more violent; an electricity lives in the air, and though I remain sealed in an environmental suit most of the time, I feel it on my skin, in my hair. And at night, a moon moves through the sky that is still the moon, but larger, closer, threatening to fall on the meadow wherever I've landed the *Aristotle*. The constellations, too, are completely different; no mythology known to humanity inhabits these night skies. I live in a museum filled with rare and exotic exhibits, and I'm afraid to even touch the glass of its display—

I know this impression makes little sense. Mine is a scientific mission, a rigorous exercise demonstrating the ingenuity of the human mind.

But it's also an artistic act, the act of a magician, conjuring magical beasts from an unfamiliar cauldron.

I believe that's why killing these animals has profoundly affected me. I feel as if I'm slaughtering living works of art.

Or perhaps I'm beginning to exhibit signs of psychological distress. Dr. Averest warned me to monitor anomalous symptoms in my reactions to my isolation. Retreat to the Viworld programs, he instructed, or let the surgical unit adjust your intercel micromeds. The drugs released by the micromeds are potent, and I've used them to best effect, but my perceptions must remain clear, unclouded by psychotropics.

But something keeps me from retreating into the virtual paradigms of the Viworld interface in the ship. While psychic interfaces perfectly render an experience of my own time, of people, of places in that time, I don't consider it a retreat, not after experiencing the magnificent alienness of the world in which I find myself. If I'm to be completely truthful, my distaste for the world I left behind is one of the most prominent reasons why I volunteered for a one-way, and permanent, journey into the past.

I really don't understand my feelings, or what's been happening to me since my arrival. Perhaps it's an inevitable consequence of the temporal transformation.

Day 200

The saurian juvenile represented the final subject of the project.

Using the ship to jump from one distant location to another across the continent has afforded me the opportunity to record a great variety of specimens, from the hills and interior forests, to shorelines and shallow seas, to deep freshwater lakes. And the Cretaceous flora and fauna I've discovered in these areas has proven remarkable, far beyond the small percentage of organisms recorded in fossils.

These animals, a herd of perhaps thirty adults and juveniles, were of a species I couldn't immediately identify, though their characteristics were similar to those familiar to paleontologists: massive bodies supported by powerful legs, thick muscles supporting long, highly responsive necks and tails, moving alongside an inland lake while feeding on the lush vegetation by the waters. Their inter-group ballet prevented the juveniles from injury, though, based on evolved instincts I could only imagine. I dared not approach their numbers in my environmental suit—even one miscalculation might see me annihilated by a leg as wide in circumference as a mature oak tree, so I refrained from testing those instincts and monitored their movements from my ship.

I used the ship's defensive weapons to neutralize the juvenile.

The rest of the herd paused where it fell, and I could only wonder if their inquisitive nosing of its carcass held any emotional reaction—again, I found myself anthropomorphizing, feeling their loss in a very human way even if they could not. After a while the herd moved on along the lake shore, leaving the dead juvenile for scavengers.

That *I* was that scavenger was a grim fact not lost on my conscience.

I left the ship where I'd landed, bounding effortlessly in my environmental suit, the filtering process of its atmospheric regenerator accommodating for the differences in gas percentages, before beginning tissue removal and storage for later analysis within the ship. I completed the tissue removal without incident, occasionally staring out over the calm water of the lake as ancient bird species glided over its surface, their colorful feathers flashing in the sunlight as beautifully as any I'd seen in my time.

But when I'd completed my tasks and stood gazing down on the dead juvenile, still as large as a small elephant, a terrible melancholy flooded through my body, a profound sense of guilt for having killed so elegant a creature. I walked around its body marking the defined musculature and grayish mottled skin, the large round head with large, open eyes staring lifelessly into the void, the thick tongue protruding slightly from its open jaw. Once part of a beautiful natural system in its paradisiacal world, I had killed it for the sake of a scientific imperative that wouldn't exist for millions of years.

I stood staring at the fallen saurian foolishly; scavengers would surely catch the scent of the dead animal by my side and come to investigate, placing me in unnecessary jeopardy.

But the juvenile saurian would be the last of the specimens I would encode into the final pod, along with this journal. The crystalline pods were a finite commodity, immensely difficult to create in my own time and impossible to create in this one. The finality of my project and the poor creature's death merged in my mind and froze me—in a manner of speaking, I was now as dead as the animal I'd killed.

And in that moment I remembered an incident from my childhood, in days before endless phasing of information and technical training, when I'd visited my maternal grandmother's small house in the countryside. Old in my young eyes, she grew roses on trellises fixed to the side of her house, cultivating them carefully, raising their lovely red and white blooms in the sun. I remember standing before those trellises stunned by the beauty of the vision of all those glowing flowers, and realized, even in my child's mind, that the natural beauty I beheld represented the greatest part of human existence. Death, killing, war, social strife all marred the potential of the esthetic wonder of creation.

I couldn't help myself—I pulled one of the roses from the others and sat on the grass carefully studying the bloom in my hands, fascinated, as I was always fascinated by living things. I kept that rose in my room, but, of course, it withered and blackened with decay, its beauty also blackening in my eyes. I didn't understand the consequence of removing that beautiful rose from its natural environment until much later in my life.

But by then I'd accepted the scientific process as a necessary part of my learning curve and ignored the destruction of those things I examined in my studies. My research alone on paleoneurological development required me to terminate countless animals, perfunctorily dissect their remains, and think no more of the enterprise than the washing of my hands after my labors.

I turned abruptly from the dead juvenile and scanned the distant trees for signs of predators.

Then I began moving back toward my ship, intending to hold onto the final pod while I contemplated my condition. I suspected, from my reaction to this last specimen, that something had malfunctioned in the temporal transformation process to leave me in so cluttered a state of mind. I felt it best to postpone burying the final pod until I had offered posterity my best analysis.

Day 220

With my provisions diminishing, I've activated the native food processing equipment that has until now lain dormant in the ship.

The same analyzers I've been using to copy and code specimen DNA will now filter indigenous flora into samples I'll be able to digest without poisoning myself; likewise, any animal protein I might consume will be tested for biological compatibility. Despite the millions of years, the chemical differences aren't so great that I'll be unable to find enough food to keep myself alive for the immediate future. At least, this was the plan when I volunteered to travel back through time—

The final compression pod sits on the shelf by my bunk, gleaming in the artificial light like a precious jewel. Its crystalline structure should endure the eons like stone, precious or otherwise, beneath the accumulating layers of rock, from this time to my own, to be excised from the sedimentary layers should it actually be found.

But the pod seems more like my denouement.

I keep it because I'm afraid to close that final door.

The ship has the potential to keep me alive for decades, should I resolve my sustenance issue—the stored pharmaceuticals and the Medoc will maintain my health and heal my injuries, the atmospheric filters will keep me breathing a suitable mixture of gases, the unending files of the Viworld programs will keep me entertained through all the hours of isolation through my neural implant. Yet, something is still very wrong in my mind.

The world I left is certainly a technophile's dream, and the level of technology we've achieved as an intelligent species is magnificent. To have finally mastered the energetic states of the universe within our technology should give me a sense of enduring pride, and to now exist as an important historical entry in that chronicle—but I wonder if I've been mistaken, if my motives for volunteering, along with my colleagues, were erroneously embraced. To bring back living fossils into the time of humanity has long been a fantasy of biologists, but was it wise to use our immense technology to fulfill so self-indulgent a desire?

Mastering interstellar flight gave humanity the bravado for high technological achievements—discovering the secrets of the quantum mapping of space-time gave us the ability to travel quickly between stars by utilizing the potential energy fields of the universe. Once we understood that all matter could be mapped through quantum coding and recreated as information through different dimensions of space-time, the application of the technology inevitably found its way into the concept of temporal mapping.

When I was a child, still fascinated by my grandmother's roses, Wu discovered that, while we couldn't send matter back through time in violation of the conservation laws, we *could* send information back through time in sequences coded into the energy potential field underlying space-time—the properties of entanglement caused the time-existent matter to conform to the excitation of the energy fields. Our concept of time is only relative, after all, and means nothing to the underlying energy potential of the universe. Accelerating packets of quantum-coded information through FTL dimensions finally allowed a measure of matter to be deconstructed, coded as quantum-potential, and projected into the past.

The only problem with the existing technology of my time, of course, was that the process of FTL acceleration couldn't easily be controlled, only directed at theoretical points in space, carefully calculated to coincide with estimated coordinates for past space-time localities. Matter emerged in its coded state from the energy potential field as its information had been coded—with the understanding that so much energy had to be used in order to send the information into FTL dimensions that hope of a return trip was impossible.

And so I was sent back through time, not a hundred years into the past, but nearly a hundred million years if the calculations were correct, my ship, my equipment, my stores, and my body all disassembled during the laser coding process and reassembled trillions of kilometers away along the pathway of the entanglement through FTL dimensions.

And all these things seemed to prove the theory, working as perfectly as they were designed, manifesting the *Aristotle* and its contents only slightly further out in Earth's orbit than the calculations assumed, a circumstance easily corrected by the ship's complex navigation system. My self-indulgent mission to capture specimens and code their DNA profiles into crystalline pods for far future generations to utilize in resurrecting extinct species succeeded brilliantly—

Except that I feel as if *I* wasn't reinterpreted correctly—my psychology seems affected, and perhaps that's a symptom of re-creating the thought processes of an organic entity, though the mapping process should have been accurate to the level of subatomic particles.

I find myself feeling overly sentimental about my mission, my memories, my current predicament; I can't stop envisioning my grandmother's roses in my conscious thoughts or my dreams, and I don't know why they should preoccupy me—and I still can't resolve myself to my complete and utter isolation from humanity.

This should not be the case. I was chosen for this mission *because* of my psychology, because of my predilection for solitude. I survived, alone, within module testing for a *year* without emotional distress—why should I feel so alone now?

Though I shouldn't have any trouble manifesting food, water, and entertainment for the duration, I feel, now that my mission is complete, that I have to address this emotional disconnect—I have to find a way to connect emotionally with my new environment despite my isolation.

I never had a pet as a child; but perhaps I can have one now, if I have the technical ability to create one.

Day 226

While collecting samples of vegetation for analysis (in the hope of finding a sufficient dietary for my future needs), I also studied the territory where I landed the ship for likely subjects for my experiment.

What I intend to do lies beyond the limits of my mission's protocols, but who is around to censure me? My training in paleoneurology will assist me, as well as the spare neural implant I have onboard in the event my imbedded device malfunctions. I can reprogram the Medoc to operate on a subject other than myself and use the servos in my environmental suit to move a heavy subject (though not so imposing that it could easily injure or kill its new host). The most difficult calculation will come in determining which drugs to use to sedate the creature—relying on the Medoc's knowledge of organic models might result in an overdose (killing the creature) or an under-dose (resulting in an uncooperative specimen).

I've located a family (or small herd, depending on the terminology I've found myself using to describe living dinosaur groups) of theropods occupying the local territory I'm now surveying, similar but not identical to the genus *Ornithomimus*, though these versions are much smaller than those fossil specimens known from the historical Denver Formation. This species may be a subset of the fossil record unknown to paleontologists, but in any event the adults fall into dimensions with which I'm comfortable—one meter at the hip and three and a half meters from snout to tail. This version is featherless, though it does bear a light brown camouflage of modified skin cells, and possesses great speed and agility. I'm still not certain of the method I'll use to move close enough to one to anesthetize it.

My plans are foolish, I know, and completely unscientific, but at least this project will occupy my time and keep my mind off my isolation. And, if my plan actually works, I may even find myself owning the Cretaceous equivalent of a family pet.

While the Medoc's computers were parsing floral samples, I slipped into the Viworld programs for a few hours, choosing to examine some of the many documentaries among the dramatizations. So quickly had I come to expect the vision of a completely natural world beyond the technological womb of the ship that I'd forgotten some of the wonders of my own time, the beautiful cities, the Viworld reality of everyday life, the grand starships returning from their exo-planet studies carrying cargo of rare and precious elements that would continue to supply exotic human endeavors.

The very same world that created the technology used to send my information back millions of years—

The voices narrating these documentaries, though, weren't actually human voices, but artificially engineered sounds designed to provide the listener with an optimum listening experience, generated by an artificial intelligence created to replace the natural order—so even in these voices I couldn't find human companionship, only a blatant reminder that I was still alone, very much alone in a world not my own.

Day 241

The ornithomimid of my experiment sleeps outside the ship during the night, forages for food and water in the daytime, but returns to the *Aristotle* without difficulty.

The initial surgical procedure seemed to proceed without incident, though wrestling an unconscious theropod onto the ship proved challenging enough for the capabilities of my environmental suit. The initial anesthetization didn't prove fatal to the creature, as I feared, though keeping it unconscious did prove precarious—had it awakened inside the ship it may have caused irreparable damage in its panic.

The Medoc accepted my programming without incident and performed the implantation of the neural interface unit into the base of the animal's skull as if it were a human being. Prior to the implantation, I scanned the animal's neurophysiology thoroughly to ensure I would be placing the sub-probes into its cerebellum and cerebrum properly; subsequent testing verified control over its reflexive functions.

The cognitive interface meant nothing to a non-sentient animal, of course, as it would a human being, but then, I'd learned nothing from my brief observations of saurian communication except that they used posturing and sound production in nearly identical ways as creatures of my time. This species of *Ornithomimus* produced clicking and percussive notes reminiscent of trumpeting bird calls, though each creature's interpretation of the sounds they heard remains a mystery. Perhaps if I knew, I could train it to respond to spoken commands, but that's probably an unrealistic fantasy.

I've managed, once I removed the creature from the ship, to begin training it through neural stimulation, and only once had to induce catatonia when it seemed to be moving toward me with hostile intentions (probably initiated by defensive instincts). I've also managed to induce dopamine production for preferred behavior, such as providing a low-level euphoria when it remains near the ship, and olfactory cues for purposes of navigation—the creature possesses an extraordinary sense of smell, one that may prove useful in the field. Teaching the animal to associate a given odor to a given dopamine level keeps it returning to the Aristotle, and will, at least for as long as I can keep producing this artificial scent.

So far, my training has proven as effective as I could hope for, given my limitations in understanding the animal's neurophysiology. But I must let it feed and water itself, since I'm only marginally capable of providing native food supplies for even myself. The creature is primarily carnivorous, dining on small animals and insects, though it will eat berries and other seeds, perhaps as a way of supplementing its diet.

I've been sampling the approved flora my processors have refined, though a strictly vegetarian diet of bland plants will not satisfy my gustatory needs for long. I'm including new fruits and roots for analysis, hoping to be able to create my own soup and stew recipes for regular consumption. I've yet to eat available animal protein.

I've named my Ornithomimid *Iddi*—an abbreviation for *idiosyncratic*. Iddi is male, by the way—sexing a theropod is nearly identical to sexing most reptiles, if only bizarre by context. When he stands, he regards me like a cross between a hairless kangaroo and an ostrich, though he is much longer and more muscular than either. His head is small and avian, and though this species is essentially featherless he does possess a hide surprisingly fur-like in texture and mottled with varying dark and light patches perfectly acquired for stealth. His large eyes hold a slightly pinkish hue and observe the world keenly. When he stares at me, I'm not really certain what he believes he sees—I imagine his perceptions are typical for an animal of his neurologic development.

Iddi seems inclined to spontaneous exhibitions of running, like an athletic dog joyously loping across a field. His presence has raised my spirits immeasurably.

Once I have him sufficiently trained, I'll begin my next endeavor, a pursuit evolved from another fascination—

At some location on this continent lies the ancestor of the roses which grew on my grandmother's trellises—I intend to find it, analyze and confirm its lineage, and know for myself the progenitor of such beauty, the mother plant of all the roses ever known to art and science of humanity. I feel, inexplicably, that this connection will bring me to my own sense of belonging.

Day 251

I have to admit that my poetic appreciation of the family Rosaceae has presented prosaic problems I hadn't anticipated.

The Genus *Rosa*, from which the rose of my time originated, is replete with a variety of types of flowering plants, and tracing the ancestral roots of one of its offshoots has proven entirely frustrating given the nearly unrecognizable species of my contemporary world.

I began my expedition by preparing a reference model of the general rose genome as represented by *Rosa chinensis*, a beautiful and complex DNA graph existing in the ship's computer library. Its completeness, gifted researchers by Finley's quantum laser scanning techniques, can easily be broken into component scaffolds against which I can test prospective species for commonalities, though those commonalities will surely appear in other species of the Rosaceae. Before Finley's chemical signature scanning, researchers had to rely on incomplete sets of configurations, thus limiting their efforts in paleobotanical studies. Though fossils of my era only traced the modern rose species to forty million years prior, given the limitations of morphological studies in rock, I'm convinced that a true ancestral line *must* exist, either in the part of the future-historical North American continent on which I now reside or elsewhere in the world.

I am endeavoring, therefore, to find a genetic needle in a global haystack.

My initial attempts at locating this ancestral line remain limited to visual identification of possible subjects and subsequent genetic analysis, a tedious and time-consuming activity. Though with nothing else to occupy my time in a planet bereft of human interests, I may as well resign myself to an extremely long-term study. So far I've failed to find any trace of the line, though I have yet to expand my search area to other parts of the continent.

I plan to bring Iddi along with me despite the technicalities.

I've grown accustomed to his company, as bizarre as that may seem to anyone of my time; keeping a dinosaur as a 'pet' lies beyond the scope of my mission, but his presence has contributed greatly to maintaining my sanity in my solitude. I've continued to train him to respond to my commands, and he's accompanied me on several excursions into the forests and hills. He possesses an uncanny sense for potential predators and responds to threatening sounds reflexively, giving me the impression I'm in the company of a well-trained bird dog. He's also proficient at rooting out hidden fauna, smaller bird species and mammals hiding in the undergrowth. I'm continually amazed by the diversity and abundance of animals in this world and mournful that the fossil record of my time only acknowledged a small percentage of their numbers.

Despite my reliance on Iddi for companionship, I've lately begun second-guessing my decision to alter his brain function in order to accommodate my personal needs— yesterday, as we stood together outside the ship admiring the brilliant sunrise, he seemed to suffer an odd seizure during which he collapsed onto the grass and lay violently trembling, his long tail whipping dangerously in the air and his neck writhing like an agitated snake. I scanned his neural processes after this seizure subsided, but without proper neurological references for his species, or any of the *Ornithomimus* species, the resulting data seemed senseless. Iddi recovered brightly, though, rising from the grass and studying the world—and myself—curiously before running off to ostensibly drink, or eat, or both. Later, he returned without incident and slept outside the ship as usual.

But the incident disturbed me. I can't help feeling an unsettling guilt over the situation, as if I've sacrificed the animal's physical integrity simply to supply myself with a canine facsimile. Iddi's unique talents in the field justify my alteration of his neurology to some degree, but I remain ambivalent about my actions. I've put the matter from my mind for the time being, focusing instead on my strategy for locating the rose ancestor in other parts of the world.

Day 266

Despondency is a heavy hand; it can lay on your shoulder or it can close around your throat and choke your breath away.

I repeatedly anesthetized Iddi and transported us from one location on the continent to another, each time leaving the ship to explore the local flora in search of likely candidates for my studies. Iddi followed reluctantly, discomfited by the unfamiliar terrain, constantly sniffing at the air and gazing warily at the trees and fields. While I collected samples, carefully cataloging plant types and coordinates, my *Ornithomimus* guarded our site, his tail moving slowly in response to sounds, alternately rising high on his muscular legs and then crouching on his forelimbs as he licked suspiciously at the ground.

I felt my mania growing daily—my desire to find the ancestor of the rose has me hurrying toward any new dicotyledonous variety I detect, certain that *this* time I'll achieve my goal. But despite the hundred or so samples I've taken, none correspond to the rose genome of my model. I've discovered several new species unknown to paleobotany, but this achievement fails to raise my spirits.

I find myself retreating into the Viworld programs in the evenings, trying to balance my current reality with a vision of the life I once enjoyed, if I ever enjoyed that life. But I find satisfaction in neither world.

Though I have a fortune in high technology at my disposal, my use of it seems pointless—as does my arbitrary decision to search for so elusive a species. I'm beginning to question my sanity.

Two days ago, Iddi and I stood afield listening to the distant bellowing of a herd of hadrosaurs beyond the trees; soon after their trumpeting diminished with their movements, Iddi fell to the grass suffering another seizure. He remained incapacitated much longer this time, though he eventually recovered and followed my environmental suit slowly back to the ship.

I've made an unforgivable error placing a neural implant into Iddi's brain—subsequent scans indicated cell death in his cerebellum, a state of affairs that will surely worsen over time. I've kept him sedated in the ship, watching over him like a sick pet, trying to devise a way in which to return him to the wild. I have to believe I only mean to alleviate my own feelings of guilt for having turned him into my version of a boon companion.

I'm not entirely certain, but I believe I can remove the implant and heal the damage done, though I can't reverse the cellular death that's already occurred. My hope is that he'll retain enough of his neural capacity to live out a natural lifespan.

I plan to return to the area where I found him, perform the implant removal, and release him into the wild once he's recovered.

Then I'll continue my search for my nascent rose alone.

Day 270

Iddi is dead.

After flying the ship back to Iddi's forest I engaged the Medoc for the necessary surgical reversal on his brain.

Initially, the implant removal seemed successful, but after an hour my poor *Ornithomimus* began suffering grand mal seizures, his respiration began failing, and so I instructed the Medoc to proceed with euthanization.

While securing DNA samples for my mission, I'd destroyed hundreds of animals, some incredibly beautiful species, and yet felt no emotional distress over the process. But for Iddi's death I felt the last of my composure crumble like an old house laid waste by erosion. I wept like a child losing a beloved dog, hating myself for having created the circumstances of his death. Instead of removing his body to the wild to be consumed naturally, or vaporizing his remains with intense microwave energy, I carried Iddi's body from the ship, spent an inordinate amount of time excavating a deep enough pit, and laid his remains in the earth as if I were burying a family member.

As I stood over Iddi's 'grave' I understood, too, that I had created just that in my mind—a facsimile of a human friend to maintain the illusion I wasn't all alone in this world.

When I volunteered for my mission I understood the implications of arriving on a world uninhabited by any other intelligent being—of finding myself alone and without the resources to return should my circumstances prove untenable. I'd been supplied with an artificial environment capable of supporting my life for many years, pharmaceuticals to attend to any psychological distress, more virtual references than I could possibly review in a normal lifetime—and yet, I had fallen victim to the depression and despair from which my psychology had been identified as being indemnified. But why?

My mission is essentially complete, the experiment has proven a resounding success, I have comported myself as perfectly as any scientist conducting extraordinarily important research. Why should I lose control of my perceptions after arriving in so inhuman a world?

Before I complete the placement of the final pod I feel I must answer this question as rationally as possible for those who may find it in the millions of years to come.

And while I deconstruct my fragile conscience, I'll continue my search for the ancestor of the rose.

There *is* an answer—

Day 285

In the days following Iddi's death, I contemplated my ambivalent feelings even as I prepared coordinates to move the ship across the ocean to continue my search on another continent.

I kept reviewing Viworld programs, reacquainting myself with the breadth of human history and achievement in order to remind myself of the reality from which I'd traveled so far from in time.

No other species in our known universe has mastered the physical world as has humanity, no other species has utilized science and technology to change the natural world in ways that benefited our needs. To have conquered disease, to have traveled to other worlds, to have created an intellectual panoply on which to decorate our definition of existence—no other living organism can claim as much, no other species' intelligence can offer as many achievements. Why should I feel intimidated by a world occupied only by animals of limited intelligence?

Human beings have demonstrated an ability to master every natural challenge they've encountered in their history.

Why shouldn't I carry on this tradition of environmental exploitation, even in my solitude?

Given the technology in my hands, I should be able to easily manipulate time and space to fulfill my needs, whether physical or psychological.

So I resolved to continue my travels in search of the ancestor of my grandmother's roses despite my feelings over Iddi's death.

Rising into orbit and falling down again onto the unfamiliar continental configurations gave me a sense of purpose, as did skimming over the mountains and shallow continental seas as I scanned the flora for flowering plants. And every time I detected a likely candidate for my nascent rose, I descended, donned my environmental suit and stalked the landscape feeling empowered by the high technology I employed.

I moved through one environmental exhibition after another, measuring the atmospheric warmth unknown in my time, examining new forests, swamps, savannas, and plains, gathering specimens and reviewing their genetic profiles aboard ship.

Failing to find the correct profile didn't dishearten me; I knew it would only be a matter of time before I and my impressive technology located the precise plant species. The high intelligence and grand technology of human beings, unknown to any other species on Earth, were capable of untold technical miracles.

But it was only while observing the maneuvers of ancient white birds in an azure sky, having failed once again to locate my rose, that I realized that no human-born engineering could compare to the beauty and perfection of the natural world.

Those birds were flying aloft in a sky no other human beings had ever seen, perfectly constructed and perfectly attuned to the world, masters of their environment even without sublime science and technology. As I stood in my grotesque environmental suit, a bulky imitation of natural function, I realized that I and humanity were not masters of the natural world, we were only pale imitations of a natural perfection seeking to control the very elements from where we emerged millions of years prior.

I had come to the past on the wings of applied physics, reincarnated in a prehistoric world, engineered by the future but constructed of the elemental particles of prehistory. In my time, we had been under the impression that we were the pinnacle of natural selection, that our intelligence gave us the mantle of superior species—but we weren't superior, only self-aware.

I had come to the past to use exotic technology to preserve the genetic profiles of extinct species so that the science of my time could resurrect lost flora and fauna—but for what purpose? To what end?

The Earth of my time had been slowly losing its own extant species ever since human beings began razing the planet like industrious ants. What is the point of proving a thing can be achieved technologically if the world perishes of the proof?

The world in which I now find myself is an extraordinarily beautiful paradise, free of human intrusion, except for myself.

And what have I done during my stay, the only human being on the planet, but kill living creatures for the sake of an experiment that has practically no chance of succeeding? Corrupting a living animal to assuage my loneliness and needlessly taking its life? Using profound technology in a vain search for the genetic precursor to a flower special only in one man's memory?

I am the pinnacle of human expression in a world without any need of it.

But now that I've answered the question that's been

plaguing me since my arrival, what's to be done?

Day 365
My search is over.

Not that I've accomplished my goal—I've actually abandoned it in light of the events of the previous day.

After returning to the proto-North American continent to begin my search again, believing that I'd simply overlooked the proper species in the area that would become the badlands in my time, I happened to encounter a group of foraging *Ornithomimus* in the coniferous forests; I stood in my environmental suit, a solitary figure in a large world, observing these animals move like dancers through the foliage, their bright eyes gleaming in the sunlight, perfectly attuned to the music of their world.

And suddenly I no longer cared about the rose or its antecedents.

I was overcome by the beauty of the animals I witnessed in their natural world, an esthetic wonder that easily supplanted my memory of my grandmother's roses. These were living expressions of beauty, and I could only corrupt them by intruding on their reality with my own.

I intend to close the final pod of my mission and bury it as planned. Perhaps someone will actually find it in years to come, and interpret these words, and know their meaning. I find it difficult to describe such beauty in any language, but perhaps they will glean some meaningful impression.

I know my fate is to go extinct, just as all the creatures I've seen during my mission, and I'll never see my own time again. I am a singular species in a world not my own. But perhaps I can still hope that, through my efforts and the efforts of others performing similar missions, this world may live again, however briefly.

I simply don't belong in this world, this beautiful world untainted by human influence. Resplendent plants and animals decorate this world, and singing birds, and beautiful flowers. So many beautiful flowers in this sacred place.

They will mark my grave.

Some Time After the Apocalypse: Family Loyalty, Part I
Terrie Leigh Relf

Ripe pears and fresh greens,
cherries tart, sans pits,
an avocado with salsa fresca,
and yes, she consumes them all,
our own hungers gnawing
through our very bones.

"More!" she cries, as if our gardens
were fertile with organic fruit,
with vegetables sure to ripen
destined for her gluttonous maw.

She is our older sister
(as we are so oft reminded),
and so must do our part,
as she has always claimed
the inalienable, "Me first!"

Until it is our time (if ever),
we sprinkle salt, store fragrant herbs
prepare the spit and sharpen knives.
For our patience a just reward:
We'll soon make a feast of her.

Mechanical Mannequins
Priya Sridhar

Effie's tiny boots echoed against the backstage wooden boards. Her head drooped, and she studied the cracks between the floorboards. Each step carried a finality, about the burden that she was carrying.

"So you see, Ms. Euphemia, your measurements might have changed over the years, but we can adjust that," the seamstress manager Josiah was saying. "We can easily cut her down to size."

Once, Effie's belly had been rotund, and she had to keep hiding the evidence of her penchant for sweets and soft drinks. That had changed. She was now so skinny that her corset's whalebones seemed to rattle against her ribs as she moved. Her pea-green eyes had dark circles under them, and some melancholy that dimmed their cheer. She kept her hair up in a chignon that she hadn't rolled properly, and threatened to fall apart.

Mannequins drooped from their pedestals. She sat and studied them. Each was painted a light shade of brown, the color of syrup. There was one mannequin that Effie recognized; it had a carved face with a slanted nose, identical to hers. It also had wide hips, and a length in the beginning indicating a paunch. She came forward.

"Hello," she said quietly. "It's been a while, hasn't it?"

The mannequin was her height and stood on a black pedestal. Coiled wires bound her to tiny supports, keeping her upright. Effie remembered standing on a stool and posing for hours; her arms and legs had tingled under her many petticoats.

"She's been well-oiled. She has been remarkable for mimicking your pose and gestures," Joziah explained. "And we can easily remove the parts which approximated your . . . previous figure. You look good now."

"No," she said. "I think that she is fine the way she is."

"Then what about your measurements? She won't be any use if she isn't accurate."

Effie had to stop and consider that. She swore that though the mannequin had no eyes, that its face twisted towards her, ever so slightly. The pedestal didn't expel steam, which meant that no power went through it, but she sensed that it was trying to meet her gaze. Some sort of reassurance came through.

"I guess we will have to adjust her," she said reluctantly. "It may take some time though. Can I come and visit her again?"

"You may," Joziah said. "Your family has been one of our best customers. You are welcome to see the mannequin until she is done. Then she may be reassigned."

Day after day, Effie walked the three blocks to the sewing shop. Joziah recognized her, as did the other seamstresses. Part of her longed to join them in their mundane work, but she knew that would never do. Her family would die if she decided to work long hours to craft dresses at a pittance. The morning chill would make her curls cling to her head, and they would stand on end if she undid all of her hairpins.

Effie would walk to the storeroom in the back. She would thread her needle, tie it off smartly, and then focus on the cloth. This was going to be a sealskin cap, one that would keep her niece warm. She pressed the needle through the thick, tanned hide, and she would have to yank it through. The stitches were large and uneven. She had to redo them, over and over again. The sealskin scraps would go on the day's newspaper, which had more editorials about the worries of mechanical mannequins that serve as models.

"I thought he would be the one," she told her mannequin. "Really, Mannequin Effie, you'd expect that a boy from a reputable family would be honorable enough to plan for the vows. But he had to go off on that journey and then decided that our engagement wasn't worth it. I hate him so much for it, for taking our future from me."

The mannequin stood stiffly on the pedestal. Effie leaned against her. She knew this was against protocol, but she had been sewing in an uncomfortable position for hours. The mannequin room had no chairs, and she didn't dare ask. There was no room for it. Joziah might well demand her to leave.

"The worst part is that my family had been expressing doubts, but they never openly opposed the engagement. He had enough inheritance and enough breeding. As soon as his father sent the letter demanding that I return the ring, my mother and father were so commiserating. They said that I would find someone better. Then on top of the company that was going to sponsor my work apprenticeship going under, it left me adrift. My work mistress liked me, but she couldn't save me from the chop. That's why I came home as soon as it was clear that I wasn't going to have lodgings abroad to prepare my work or plan for a wedding."

Effie closed her eyes. She could feel the mannequin breathing against her silent sisters.

"Some days, Mannequin Effie, I wish I could switch places with you. You know your place, where you need to be. And you could live my life, and know exactly what to do with it."

She fiddled with the tiny switch on Mannequin Effie's pedestal. It was an oval knob, the kind that was used for kerosene lamps. She flipped it. Steam emerged from the pedestal's vents.

Mannequin Effie shivered. The kerosene lamps made her polished wood glisten. She started to move, shaking out wooden fingers that tiny wires connected. Effie stood up and away from her, just enough to give the mannequin some space. She stepped on the newspaper, crinkling an anti-machine editorial.

"Oh Mannequin Effie," she whispered. "You are beautiful the way you are. I wish that you wouldn't have to exist just so they know how I look, all the time."

The mannequin lifted its hand. Effie stood still. Her breath caught in her throat. Mannequin Effie reached for her hair. Effie waited.

Wooden hands started pulling the hairpins out. Effie's chignon fell completely apart. She caught the pins as they fell. Then fingers combed through her hair, straightening it.

"Oh Mannequin Effie," she whispered. Tears streamed down her face, streaking her rouge. She stood and let the tears fall, daring not to make a sound. The mannequin petted her head gently.

*   *   *

"Ah, Ms. Blackstamp." The woman sitting behind the desk nodded at Effie. The nameplate at her desk read RUTH SIMON. "We were happy to call you in for this interview. Please tell us about yourself."

Effie sat up straight. She wore a new dress from Joziah's shop, sewn from black silk with a grey lining. It fit perfectly over her corsets, which had not rattled once.

"My degree was in the mechanical sciences," she said. "These recommendations come from my professors. I studied for several years and also took a brief apprenticeship at Lord Steam's Aeronautics. I contributed to several projects, including preliminary tests on mechanical captains for cargo ships. My skills lie in making projections for the future; my results were eighty percent accurate when crafting plausible hypotheses. I can also make large calculations rapidly."

"I see. And you are not worried about the fears of these mechanical beings gaining unwanted life, and overturning our rule, Ms. Blackstamp? It has been the talk of the papers."

Effie thought of the mannequin she had purchased with a handful of coins from her inheritance. Joziah had said that Mannequin Effie would be a sore loss from his shop, but he would happily design another if Effie wanted future dresses. Effie planned to pay for Mannequin Effie's replacement so that her family wouldn't ask questions.

"That depends on if we treat these mechanical beings with respect," she said. "We make them serve us, but we have to remember that they provide many good deeds in exchange for their existence. As long as we are intelligent and kind, as I have seen in my research, then we have nothing to fear. And I can see that your company respects these beings. That is why I want to work for you."

Ruth Simon blinked. Her desk had several playbills that read THE METAL BALLET COMPANY. SWAN LAKE, 8 PM. COME SEE AUTOMATIC MARVELS, NEVER BEFORE SEEN!

"Yes, we do," she said. "And you are available to start as soon as next week?"

"Yes," Effie said. "I would be happy to work in your various departments, in the position."

Ruth wrote down notes. She didn't smile when she said the next few words, but there was relief in her tones.

"You will be expected first to shadow our team of mechanics. I will introduce you to the team on Friday, and I suspect you shall get along. With the season starting, we need all the help we can get to get high turnouts for our shows. Your wages will be two hundred a week."

"Thank you, Ms. Simon," Effie said. She gave a smile that hid all the excitement she was feeling. "I will be happy to start at the Metal Ballet Company."

She wondered if she could take Mannequin Effie to the theater, and treat her to a show. But that would be for later. For now, she had to build her life back together and make sure her curls were properly pinned in place.

Understudies
By Priya Sridhar

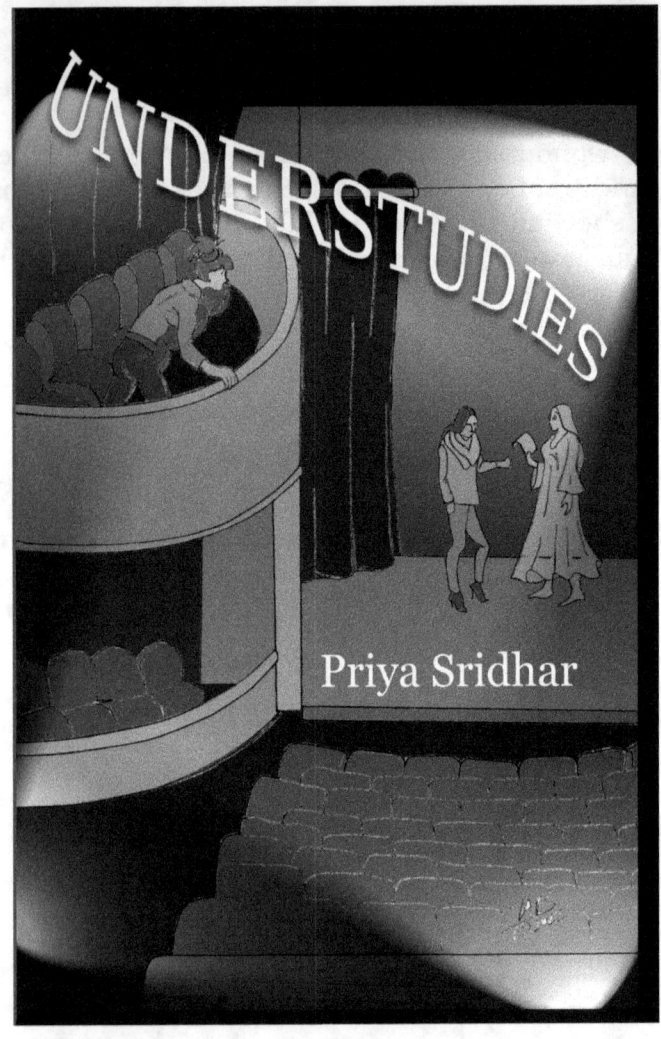

The Stardust Sisters have always made their parody shows work. So what if they lost their third member to Hollywood? Does it even matter that they don't have a new theater facility? Grad school should fix that, twin sisters Stella and Evangeline calculate, and they'll get the funding, as well as a decent apartment in the city.

As if by miracle, an apartment with no rent opens up—in the Haunted Basilio Theater, where new management wants a fresh start after summer camp went wrong. All the twins have to do is perform a show scripted a century ago, and give up bits of their body heat. The show must go on, right? Right?!

Type: Spooky paranormal novella
Audience: adults

Ordering Links:
Print: https://www.hiraethsffh.com/product-page/understudies-by-priya-sridhar
ePub: https://www.hiraethsffh.com/product-page/understudies-by-priya-sridhar-2
PDF: https://www.hiraethsffh.com/product-page/understudies-by-priya-sridhar-1

The Beasts of Night
Sandy DeLuca

She waited...
into the hour of beasts...
when they emerged from twilight's shadows.

Men donned in tattered capes,
women in black lace dresses,
leaves and pebbles clung to fabric.
Eyes filled with wisdom,
hellish revolution...
hunger.

That flesh—
marble-like, shimmering
as the moon peeked through twisted wood.

They sang and danced,
spiraling with the wind,
as though they could touch the sky...
soaring into inky blackness...
then through delicate strands of moonlight...
elegant...
yet not alive—
not like a young girl who watched.

They chanted, *"Hecate, Morrigan, Freya, Hades..."*

Becoming one with dusty snow...
   a late-night horror flick come to life—

They don't know I'm here, she thought.
But she was wrong.
Because a handsome boy,
almond eyes and blue-black hair,
hovered above her...
a finger pressed to pale lips,
as she crept home.

Don't be afraid...

Yet fear consumed her,
shivering,
counting steps toward shelter.

He gazed at her,
inquisitive,
shyly, looking away at times.

His arms and legs dangled like a marionette's,
allowing the breeze to carry him
through snarled boughs.

He ascended upward
turned to smoke,
then reappeared,
coattails catching the wind,
red droplets falling to earth.

He swooped down, his lips touched her neck,
a kiss,
soft and terrifying...

He caressed her cheek,
and she knew that he could end her life...
as she gazed into those eyes,
sinking into his spell of immortality

Don't fear me...

He released her, floating up once more...

Go...

Dreading that he might still hurt her,
she ran,
finally tumbling into her open window,
quickly slamming it shut.

And he'd followed…
peered through glass…
suspended his unearthly body in winter's dark,
smiled with crimson-slashed lips,
tilted his head from side to side…

His hair—
like black ribbons, sparkled with raindrops.
So beautiful,
And he sang to her in a language she could
not comprehend,
pressing those dead hands against frosty panes…
she did the same…
fingers trembled.

And she looked into his eyes again,
wisdom and concern
soothed her, filled her with awe.
so, without dread,
she told him, "I want to be like you."

His smile widened slowly, revealing sharp fangs,
blood bubbled from his lips…

You can't be like me…
I am a beast of night…
you'll never be alone in darkness…
but know that I can't live in your light.

Then he was gone, swallowed up by vapor…
somber in his darkness…

back to an undead world…

The Uber Cat and Dragon Owner Manual by Marge Simon and Mary Turzillo
Reviewed by Lisa Timpf

Readers who have been seeking the ultimate manual on the care and feeding of pet dragons and magical cats need look no further. In *The Uber Cat and Dragon Handbook: A Pet Owner's Guide,* authors Marge Simon and Mary Turzillo offer all the necessary advice in a succinct and humorous manner.

The book is organized into sections, such as "Choosing Your New Pet," "Exercise," "Grooming," and other helpful topics. The pieces themselves come in a variety of forms, including poems, illustrations, flash fiction, and humorous articles purporting to be non-fiction. There are even lists, like Turzillo's "More Ways to Tell If Your Cat Is a Space Alien, " which includes indicators such as, "You find long distance charges on your telephone bill to area codes the operator has never heard of," and, "You come home to find your cat walking on the ceiling, and your cat just looks at you and says, 'Yeah, so?'"

Some of the poems are satirical takes on familiar songs. One such, Simon's "Streets of Toledo (The Dragon's Song)" includes the lines:

> Oh, pray you must tell me now where is your owner
> and pray tell me true did you lose all his dough?

Turzillo's "Invisible Cat," a poem about a phantom feline, contains a haunting note: "Phantom feline lives with you / He eats your food, he haunts your flat." "The Hunter's Mothers," also by Turzillo, portrays life from a cat's perspective:

> She cut meat that she had caught
> somewhere, and put it on plates as big as me
> for her other kitttens, the large bald ones.

But she never let me have the knife,
nor let me play with the meat. Was I unworthy?

In "Your Darling New Dragon" Turzillo sagely reminds owners, "Remember, that cute dragon chick dragging your station wagon around as a pull-toy will very quickly become a playful forty-foot adolescent." In the "Training Dragons" section, Simon advocates the following method for teaching a dragon to lie down as a precursor for flight training: "Using a dragon dummy, gently lower it to a prone position. Then pretend to get on it. This has worked in 1 out of 10,000 cases, but stick with it. Sooner or later, the dragon will get the connection."

Though *The Uber Cat and Dragon Handbook* was first published more than ten years ago, I only ran across it recently. The book is fairly short—just under 70 pages—but it packs a lot in a small space. As a former cat owner, I found the cat pieces to be dead-on, and the dragon lore fits with how I might imagine dragon behaviour. Witty and satirical, *The Uber Cat and Dragon Handbook* provides fun fodder for feline fans and dragon devotees.

Ordering link:

https://www.hiraethsffh.com/product-page/uber-cat-dragon-owner-manual-by-marge-simon-mary-turzillo

Movie Review: Prey
Lee Clark Zumpe

Action heroes come in a variety of shapes and sizes, with equally varying temperaments and levels of emotional complexity. The broad range in action-film protagonists can be attributed to contemporary cultural trends. What moviegoers expect from their escapist heroes — or what Hollywood believes they expect — shapes the lead characters that step up to save the day. That cinematic tenet has been true for more than a century, and it is demonstrated once again in the new film "Prey," directed by Dan Trachtenberg.

We'll get back to "Prey" shortly, after I indulge in a topical digression.

A speedy deep dive into cinema history reveals how action heroes have changed to suit each decade's mores. During the Great Depression in the 1930s, audiences turned to the likes of Johnny Weissmuller in the Tarzan franchise and Errol Flynn in various swashbuckling roles with a bit of romance thrown in for good measure. Films of the 1940s often revolved around common men called upon to make extraordinary sacrifices on the battlefields of World War II, starring actors such as Gregory Peck and Robert Mitchum. Moving in to the 1950s and 1960s, Hollywood found action hero roles in Westerns and other historical settings for an array of actors including Kirk Douglas, Anthony Quinn, John Wayne, Charlton Heston, James Dean, and Marlon Brando.

By the 1970s, the antihero had displaced the clean-cut common man in a string of popular films. Clint Eastwood introduced us to Harry Callahan in "Dirty Harry" while Charles Bronson gave us Paul Kersey in "Death Wish." Another unconventional hero debuted in 1979 in an Australian post-apocalyptic action film: Mel Gibson starred as Max Rockatansky in "Mad Max."

Then, the 1980s arrived and something weird happened: The net worth of an action hero somehow became directly connected to the circumference of their biceps. Brawn surpassed attitude, honor, and intellect as the defining characteristic of action film protagonists. The leading characters of the films got bigger, burlier, more muscular and more obsessed with victory at all costs. Yes: I'm talking about Sylvester Stallone. Yes, I'm talking about Arnold Schwarzenegger. And, to a lesser degree, I'm talking about folks like Jean-Claude Van Damme, Dolph Lundgren, and Steven Seagal. Many of the characters these actors portrayed during this period were driven, courageous, and superhuman. They also sometimes came across as unyielding, obsessed, and maybe a bit toxic.

I recently watched the 1987 science fiction-horror-action film, "Predator." Schwarzenegger stars as Major Alan "Dutch" Schaefer, a Vietnam War veteran who leads a military rescue party into a Central American rainforest to track down a foreign cabinet minister and his aide who are being held captive by insurgents. Unbeknownst to Dutch and his testosterone-fueled band of commandos, an alien lifeform has chosen the very same patch of rainforest to do some recreational hunting — kind of the intergalactic equivalent of pudgy, wealthy businessmen going on trophy game hunting vacations in Africa for the opportunity to blast holes in endangered species from a safe distance.

"Predator" doesn't disappoint if you like your action heroes beefy and indomitable. Most of the soldiers fall victim to the alien, dying horrible deaths that evoke little to no compassion. There is no depth to these one-dimensional characters, and little backstory beyond what their stereotypes imply. The script, written by brothers Jim and John Thomas, features some cringe-worthy dialog.

Still, the film, directed by John McTiernan, is satisfying enough and builds to a tense climax pitting Dutch against a formidable foe with an arsenal of high-tech alien weaponry. The film owes much of its success to special effects guru Stan Winston who contrived the creature effects. That, combined with the innovative visual effects that gave the alien thermal vision and an invisibility cloak, made Dutch's adversary seem invincible.

"Predator" did extremely well at the box office and spawned a franchise that has endured for 35 years. The initial film was followed by "Predator 2," using a different cast, in 1990. Two additional sequels include "Predators" in 2010 and "The Predator" in 2018. The Predator franchise and the Alien franchise collided for a set of mashup features including "Alien vs. Predator" in 2004 and "Aliens vs. Predator: Requiem" in 2007.

That brings us back to "Prey," Trachtenberg's new prequel to "Predator." The newest addition to the franchise premiered at the San Diego Comic-Con July 21. It was released Aug. 5, 2022, by 20th Century Studios as a Hulu original film.

The biggest complaint I have about "Prey" is that it didn't have a theatrical release.

"Prey" is about as far from "Predator" as you can get in terms of character development, emotional impact, and absence of stereotypes. Trachtenberg actively disparages the reactionary machismo that pervaded 1980s action films. He delivers all the suspense and visceral gore, but he also manages to infuse genuine, compelling drama in a coming-of-age subplot.

The prequel is set in 1719 in the Northern Great Plains.

Naru (Amber Midthunder) is a young Comanche. Her mother has trained her as a healer, but she wants to be a hunter like her brother Taabe (Dakota Beavers). While hunting a deer, she witnesses what she believes is a Thunderbird — a powerful, supernatural spirit in the form of a bird that creates thunder by flapping its wings. In fact, what she witnesses is the arrival of an alien spacecraft. Believing the vision to be a sign that she is ready for her "kuhtaamia," or sacred rite of passage, she informs her brother of her intentions. Other male members of the tribe mock her, scoffing at her desire to go against gender norms and underestimating her abilities.

When a mountain lion carries off one of the tribe's hunters, Naru joins a search party. During the search, she finds evidence that an unknown predator may be stalking them. The others ignore her, but eventually they all fall prey to the alien hunter.

Naru and her brother are eventually pushed far from their home as they confront a highly evolved alien predator with a stockpile of technically advanced weapons. The final showdown underscores how mismatched these opponents are — and how the will to survive calls forth untapped resources of strength and ingenuity.

More than a few reviewers are boasting that "Prey" is the best film in the franchise since the original, or that it stands as an equal to "Predator." Please, people: It's *better* than the original, by far.

Trachtenberg checks all the boxes with "Prey." It's scary, it's action-packed, and it's relentless. It's full of gorgeous cinematography that brings the 18th century frontier to life with stunning clarity. Midthunder's portrayal of Naru is undeniably riveting. The film fits tidily into franchise continuity with a few clever easter eggs tossed in for attentive viewers.

This is the first film in the franchise that truly aspires to be something more than a simple creature feature. Beyond the obvious shift from brawny male action hero to an unproven female hunter determined to prove herself, "Prey" offers some subtle commentary on the impending genocide of indigenous peoples in North America. Naru clearly recognizes that the alien predator is not the only danger her tribe faces.

If the female protagonist or the indigenous storyline make the newest Predator franchise film too progressive for some, that's a shame. They can dig through their VHS collections searching for something that won't infuriate them to the point of trolling social media and frantically typing rants filled with as many misspellings as misogynistic slurs. Jimmy Carter said that it is a weak person — as well as a weak nation — that behaves with "bluster and boasting and rashness and other signs of insecurity."

My advice is to ignore all that negative bluster and check out "Prey" on Hulu.

INFO BOX
"Prey"
Genres: Science fiction, action, horror
Director: Dan Trachtenberg
Cast: Amber Midthunder, Dakota Beavers, Dane DiLiegro, Michelle Thrush, Stormee Kipp, and Julian Black Antelope
Release date: Aug. 5, 2022
Run time: 99 minutes
Rated: R

Context
Gustavo Bondoni

Kwiguai yawned. She couldn't believe they'd made her get up early to listen to this bore... and a physical class, no less. The school was living in the past, and the adults had completely lost touch with reality.

"Screw this," she whispered to Minaya. "Does he think we're freshmen? He could have sent us the pics and the audio instead of dragging us down here. The humid wind is seriously messing with my hair. I swear half the sea is stuck onto my head."

"Old Denne's just about to retire. I hear he turns eighty in June and they can force him out. Meanwhile, they're humoring him."

"So we have to listen to this antique so they don't have to fire him? I'm gonna complain."

"Yeah. They can't just treat us however they want. And the train... did you smell it? It was like something died in there. Oops, busted."

"Kwiguai, did you have a question?"

"No Mr. Denner," she replied with her best smile.

"Good. So, as I was saying, this statue is placed here because Savannah was one of the major slaving ports, the biggest in Georgia. King was born in Atlanta, and this was likely where his ancestors came through."

Someone up near the front, probably that suck-up Jemmai, raised his hand. "Why is his hand extended out to the sea?"

Denner smiled and Kwiguai ground her teeth. Everyone knew Jemmai was quick with his mindnet implants. He'd probably just wikied the coordinates and shouted out the first thing he saw about the statue. Of course, Denner was so old his implants probably needed solar panels. That would explain the hat, at least.

Just to be sure, she did a coordinate search. As she'd imagined, the reason for the statue reaching out across the sea was in the first para.

She sent a quick message to Jemmai: u reek.

He didn't even move—she was watching—but responded. Straight A+. U?

Denner was droning on. "His arm is extended southeast because on a hill across the ocean, there's another statue. A statue of a man named Mandela. Nelson Mandela. Along with King, he is the most famous of the twentieth century liberators. Between them, they founded the world we know today, and now, with their outstretched hands, they form a bridge across the ocean."

She quickly scanned the information about the man they were studying. History had never been hard for her, anyone with a little implant-fu could pass even the hardest history test... and they were talking about doing away with testing anyhow. It wasn't really fair to judge people on their search ability, after all. Some people were just quicker at mental commands than others.

Martin Luther King, Jr. Blah, blah, born in the 20th century, blah blah. Gave a bunch of speeches about injustice. Shot in the 20th century by one of the people who didn't want him to win. He won anyway... the article listed of all the changes that came about because of him.

The list depressed her. Some of the stuff they did two hundred and fifty years ago made the world sound like it was run by barbarians. What difference was there between the 20th century and the Middle Ages, when you got down to it? None. You couldn't really have much of a life in either era, and that was all that mattered. People in the 20th century actually cared about race? Well, that was a long time ago, and their brains were probably smaller. Old time people did a lot of dumb stuff.

Hell, she didn't even know what race she was. One of her grandparents was from Canada... did that count as something?

The article made the man out to be some kind of saint, and she shrugged. If he did everything he was supposed to have done, then he was definitely an important guy. It figured, or Denner wouldn't have been wasting his breath— what little remained of it—on telling the man's life story to a bunch of kids who couldn't care less.

She tried to find a video of the murder. That sounded like it might be fun.

Instead, she stumbled on an article which made her gasp. She gasped and zapped it to Minaya.

"Holy shit!" her friend exclaimed. "They're actually teaching people about this guy?"

She circulated it to the rest of the class, flagged as right-now-critical. Even Jemmai had the right to see this.

Everyone went very still as they scanned.

"Wait for it..." she said to Minaya. "Wait for it... and there it is."

Jemmai's hand shot up. "Did Martin Luther King actually tell his followers to drive themselves around in cars? Is it true that they drove cars instead of taking the bus... as a political statement?"

Denner froze like he'd popped a bad lollidrop. "Well, yes. Most of them walked, while some organized to drive. But you need to understand that it was a very different era. Some races were forced to ride in the back of the bus. Can you imagine that? You were forced to give up your seat just because you had a different skin color. It was safer for many people to drive cars than to walk. What would you do if someone treated you that way?"

Minaya spoke up. She never talked in class, but Kwiguai could see the signs: the tense whiteness around her lips indicated a fury that went well beyond the usual. "I most certainly wouldn't have gotten into a car and driven around. And it says that this is before cars had smog control. Is that true?"

Denner rubbed his eyes. "I really don't know. Knowing about cars is not important in this case. You need to understand the context. Everyone drove cars back then."

"Yeah. And now we're waiting for those dikes over there to finally break and flood the whole fucking state because of these people. Didn't you see what happened to fucking Holland last year? How many millions dead? How in the world could someone build a statue to these bastards?"

"This was a really good man who made life better for everyone. He changed the world."

Jemmai was into it now. His hand was up again. "What is a reverend, Mr. Denner?"

The teacher pulled at his collar. He was sweating profusely and Kwiguai smirked in satisfaction. Served him right for making them stand in this air that thought it was soup. To his credit, Denner answered. "A reverend is an ordained minister in a church."

"A church, as in organized religion?"

"Yes."

"The kind of religion that oppressed people until the Great Liberation? My mother lost an eye in the protests that freed us. She spent six months waiting for them to grow a replacement... and you've got a statue to this bastard? I'm sorry, but I'm not staying here. And I'm lodging a complaint with the school board."

"Please. You need to understand. It was a different time back then. The things you're talking about are just normal things. This statue was erected because of great things this man did. You have to judge him by the standards of his time... and you need to learn about this."

Jemmai stopped and turned to face the teacher. "Well, I'm judging you by the standards of mine. We don't need to learn about these awful, awful people. Men like that destroyed the earth and their churches enslaved the minds of literally billions of people."

And he left.

The rest of the students trickled after him, leaving Mr. Denner alone, standing beside the statue of the man he so admired.

For a second, Kwiguai felt sorry for him. He'd lived through so much that he probably didn't even recognize the world anymore. It was a good thing he'd be retiring soon. Probably sooner once Jemmai's petition gained traction—it was already circulating and gaining several vocal group adhesions.

The teacher looked sadly out at the retreating students and shook his head. Somehow, though his job was probably forfeit, she felt that the old man's pity wasn't for himself, but for them.

Whatever. Jemmai's push had already bifurcated. A group was forming to 'Help the city deal with a problematic monument'. She grinned. She couldn't believe that something like this was happening here. It always seemed to happen in sophisticated places, like when they tore down the monument to industrialism in Paris, the big steel tower.

And now Savannah. Here. The most boring place on the planet.

She wondered what it felt like to make history. The videos of that statue hitting the water would be played all over the world... forever.

People would remember what they did. It was a new feeling for her.

Kwiguai smiled.

Need something else to read?

Go here:

https://www.hiraethsffh.com/product-page/voyuese-conquistador-by-tyree-campbell

The Tenth Symphony
Matias Travieso-Diaz

Death comes knocking at your door at the most inopportune times.

Take the case of Dmitri Ivanovitch Petuleff. Not that he was young when the black robed skeleton appeared before him; no, he was in his sixties and had known for months that his liver cancer was fatal and his exit from this world was approaching. Yet the specter's appearance took him by surprise as he crouched at his piano, trying to milk a few more notes off his tired brain.

"Go away" he challenged the visitor. "I'm busy."

"It does not matter," replied the phantom inexorably. "Your heart is about to fail. Come!"

"Please, not yet! Wait just a couple of hours! I'm nearly done here!"

"Death waits for no one. I hear the same plea from just about every mortal who faces me."

"My case is different. I'm on the verge of completing a monumental achievement!"

"Which is?"

"I'm composing the last few bars of my tenth symphony. I have most of the phrases figured out in my mind. I only need to flesh them out and complete the orchestration…"

"And why can't someone else do this after you are gone?"

"Because what I want to do will provide a sublime, unexpected ending that will bind together all the main themes of the symphony and render it unforgettable. Nobody else can do this but me!"

"Assuming that is true, why does it matter? What is so special about this symphony of yours?"

"Look, I've written a lot of music in my life, including nine other symphonies. I have met some recognition and success, but I'm no Beethoven or Mahler. This work will raise me to the rank of the immortals. It will be listened to centuries after I am gone, if only I can complete these last few bars!"

"So, your vanity is what is at stake here. Right?"

"Not just my vanity. Great music elevates the souls of the people, makes their existence better while they wait for you. I'll be forgotten shortly after I am gone, but this symphony, if I get to finish it, will endure. You owe this small gift to the multitudes you'll be taking after today. Just give me at least a few more minutes!"

"I said I do not wait. But a war plane just dropped an incendiary bomb on a hospital. Many are dying in terrible agony. I must prioritize collecting those casualties. You have a few moments respite. Use them well!"

***

He sat at the keyboard and focused on the love theme from the third movement, recalling how he meant to integrate the delicate melody into the crashing finale he envisioned. His progress, however, was interrupted by a rush of memories of his beloved wife and children, lost one way or another in the tides of the years. He recalled the tender embraces, the whispered words of passion, the glowing logs in the fireplace casting points of light and shadow on their faces, the one perfect summer afternoon all five of them had spent at the shore...

He shook himself away from those thoughts and started drafting a rising motif for the strings, underscored by the brass and the timpani, when again other memories intruded: his bitter fight for acceptance at the conservatory, a fight that had ended with the grudging recognition of his talent by director Smolensky; recognition, but never full acceptance due to his mixed race, rural background, rustic manners; his eventual success...

He was still lost in reminiscences about his triumphs and failures, his loves and losses, when there was a chill in the room and the hooded figure reappeared to stand in front of the composer, still bent over the piano, his fountain pen scribbling on the manuscript paper.

"Let's go!" commanded the figure, raising a skeletal finger to summon the composer.

"No! I need more time!" implored Petuleff.

"There is never enough time!" replied Death, making an irrevocable summoning motion with its outstretched arm.

"Oh, well, maybe the memories were worth the loss..." started the man. There was the shadow of a smile on his lips as he clutched his chest and tried in vain to right himself up.

***

The nurse found Petuleff on the floor. There were cuts on his face and hands from his fall to the ground; his body was cold and rigor mortis had set in. Also on the floor was a jumble of papers, the manuscript of a score he had been working on when he suffered the fatal heart attack. One of his students picked up the loose sheets reverently and arranged them in proper order. The last page showed an irregular diagonal ink stain that ran down from the middle of the page to its edge. Upon review, it was determined that the stain originated on the incomplete last bars of the Finale, and appeared to be the start of a variation on a theme from the preceding Adagio. It was not obvious where the composer was going with this when death overtook him.

Efforts were made to correct a few errors on an otherwise polished score and add a coda, a short climax to the main body of the movement. The codas that were generated by composers and conductors were either trite or bombastic and did little to enhance Petuleff's music, other than putting a final period on an interrupted sentence. One critic likened the efforts to complete Petuleff's final symphony to adding the missing arms to the Venus of Milo: workmanlike, but uninspired attempts to match the scope of the original artist's conception.

Petuleff's tenth symphony received its premiere three months after the composer's passing. The work was well received but, perhaps encumbered by its hobbled ending, never found a place in the pantheon of everlasting classics. In generations to come, only musical archeologists would dig up the memory of Petuleff and his many compositions, including his unfinished tenth symphony.

Maybe the world was not all that worse off for the loss.

Knowing Then What I Know Now
Christian Riley

So it went like this: I was walking along the shores of Half-Moon Bay on the night of my 40th birthday, all alone under the cover of a full moon and a spiteful southern March breeze, bearing salt for my bitter eyes which cared nothing for the likes of anything other than that crisp sand between my toes. At least I was still young enough to never-mind our cold, dirty planet underneath my feet—so I told myself, as I then looked up and witnessed a moment of time and space that was both surreal and fantastic. A moment not of this reality; my reality, your reality, anyone's reality, for that matter.

I looked twice over both shoulders, searching for another witness on that stretch of sand who might be looking at the same thing I was, and also, who could possibly help support my mind, so troubled was it upon observing this glowing, really glowing, and I mean glowing hard and bright, blue archway of shimmering light stamped into the cliff-side of the beach right next to me. But I was alone. So you'll only believe half of this story, if that. Yet here it is anyway.

Slowly, I crept up to this archway and found that no, it wasn't a trick slip of light from that full moon, because as I got closer, it got brighter, and then it grew in size and shape as well, stretching down and out until it ended in the likeness of a great, bluish-green "eye", there upon that slab of dirt and sand.

And it had "features" within it as well. Features I quickly discovered were symbols of some type. Arcane symbols perhaps. Symbols not of this earth... most definitely. Symbols that spoke loud and cruel to my curious mind, so I just had to reach up and touch those damn things.

I raised my left hand and stretched my fingers out to one symbol, realizing then that it was warm. They were warm. And when my fingers finally broke ground with that one particular symbol I had aimed for, and when I traced its curvature, traced its pathway as dug out upon that cliff-side, I realized also that those symbols were *magic*.

They were magic, because somehow, in the instant of an eye blink, I was then taken far away from that piece of Half-Moon Bay, and deposited right back into that point of time there in that bathroom within that apartment we lived in when I was just thirteen years old, and I had been struggling to get ready for school because I was also being haunted from those words spoken to me just the day before by that terrible bully, Charles Miner. Those words went like this: "Tomorrow, I'm gonna beat your head in, Ratface."

Except that now, while in that bathroom, the thought suddenly occurred to me that *Wow, I'm thirteen again. I'm thirteen, and I have to get ready for school or else I might be late; and oh yeah, Charles has plans to beat me up today, but sadly, he's gonna have to change those plans because I no longer have time for his crap. I've got more important things to worry about.*

And then I went to school.

I went to school, to junior high, with my forty-year-old intellect jammed into my adolescent body, and boy was I amazed. *This was how we walked? This was how we talked and dressed? How we* got along *with each other?* A freak-show both hilarious and unsettling, which had me more distracted than I'd counted on—or didn't count on—and that too was unsettling because like I said, I had more important things to do there in school, real important things to do, because this was my second chance, right? Time to get things right for once. Make a change worthy to be proud of for yourself, Mr. Thomas Plant.

"Ratface!"

Magic brought me there for a reason, and I was sure I knew what that reason was for, since—

"Hey, Ratface!"

—since I was forty-years-old. I was forty, so there was no way in hell I could fail a test now. I had planned on getting straight A's this time around. That's right, I was gonna make my old man proud for once when I handed him, no, *shoved* him that yellow slip of paper, that little insurance policy that told him his son was such a genius, told him to—

"Get the hell over here, Ratface... It's time for that beating!"

I had more important things to do. I did, I really thought I did, but there he was anyway: Charles Miner. Charles Miner, with his big fists. Charles Miner, with his short-cropped hair and braces, and spoiled-rotten pudgy belly. Charles Miner, with that unbelievable cruelness he somehow hijacked from a third-world dictator. And then it all came back to me. How on this day, way back when I was thirteen, I let Charles Miner give me a beating, which left me scarred for years to come. Left me with scars that paled compared to the ones I'd received from the old man, because I was the fool who confessed my cowardice to him. Confessed that I let another kid whoop my ass, and that yes, his only son was a weak little shit too afraid to stand up for himself.

Charles Miner.

Charles Miner, with his bruised ribs. Charles Miner, with his broken, bloodied-up nose. Charles Miner, big tree who fell hard, right there on the blacktop of the playground, while I punched and kicked the son-of-a-bitch with all forty years of my hatred and sorrow. I pounded Charles with forty years of humiliation until he cried loud and hard for his mama, begging me to stop already...

And then, just like that, I was twenty again!

Ode to be twenty again! Hallelujah! Twenty again! Thank the Maker! Twenty years old with forty-years of experience under my belt? Out of my way, world! And how I knew I was twenty again, is because I was there on that bed in that room I rented for that one year while I threw fries at McDonald's and thought about nothing other than Friday nights (yes, I actually had those nights off) and the next order of all-beef-patty-special-sauce-lettuce-cheese-pickles-onion on a sesame seed bun with a smack on that ass and a side of poontang, thank you very much.

Her name was Tanya Millhouse, and she was my first, almost my best, definitely my favorite, with her beautiful eyes that crinkled so heavily when she laughed out loud. A dainty girl with a huge, infectious laugh that always compelled me to give her a squeeze while I looked her in those magnificent eyes, kissed her lips, brushed my hand through her hair, kissed her neck, ran my fingers down her cheek, grabbed the underside of her knee, scooped her up and down onto the bed...

Yes, I was in love. I was in love for the first time with such a beautiful woman with beautiful eyes and a beautiful laugh, and I had the time of my life for that one year—year twenty. Not twenty years, just one, when I was twenty, and Tanya was nineteen, and I was sure I'd found the girl of my dreams, my future wife, the would-be mother of my children...

The same girl who I knew wasn't, who couldn't be, the same girl I found on her knees in the storage room at work, slurping on Fred Hurley's popsicle.

Fred Hurley: McDonald's shift manager, fat son-of-a-bitch who had a wife and four kids going on eight because him and his wife were Mormons, went to church every other odd day of the week, and who preached his version of the gospel to all of us deaf kids there at work—except for Tanya of course, who just got the wet end of his righteousness.

But she *took* that end, apparently. She asked for it. She was happy to receive it, because when I caught her in that storage room with *Fred*, she looked up at me, (a little surprised, *just a little*), then looked back at him, at *it*, and then proceeded to get the job done—never-mind that her boyfriend was standing off to the side, javelin lodged deep into his ribcage...

And after that, I simply turned around and walked out of that McDonald's, remembering to drop my heart onto the griddle before I was out the door.

I went home and sat on that bed where I was now, in that same moment, thinking about how adultery stood next to murder on my list, and that my life, my future life with all its future relationships will forever be jaded by a million replays of Tanya, Fred, and The Storage Room Suck Off, and that... But wait...

I was forty now. Also. Forty, also. I was forty, and I had a whole lot more to think about regarding my future life. A whole lot more to *remember* about. So when Tanya Millhouse came calling, knocking on my window because I'd ignored all fourteen of her attempts to get me on the phone, I opened the back door which led to my part of the house and gladly let her into my room.

She had that look I remembered so very well, back when this moment first occurred twenty long years ago. That look that said, *I'm here to apologize, even though I don't want to, but... you know, it's sort of the right thing to do.*

And when she then proceeded to open her beautiful mouth, yet speak that ugly script that also had me thinking, *How the hell did Fred Hurley get in here?,* I simply couldn't take my mind off the fact that Tanya Millhouse was *only* my first. Certainly not my last, nor my best. And certainly not going to be my favorite anymore, because yeah, I was a forty-year-old man with the body of my youth, and the wisdom of my years sitting right next to me on that bed (the opposite side of where Tanya sat), tugging on my ear, whispering into my conscience, saying, *Hey Tom? Yeah, you. Why are you letting this sweet young thing break your heart? She's just a girl trying to find her way, just like all the rest of us. Give her up already.*

And wouldn't you know, it was that easy. It was so easy for me I couldn't even let Tanya finish with her apology. I just laughed softly, then rambled on to the effect of: *Don't stress over it girl, it's all cool, I'm alright, there're tons of fish in the sea, no worries, oh, but by the way, maybe you should reconsider this thing with Fred Hurley though... I believe I read somewhere that those Mormon women can get awfully 'vengeful when it comes to cheating matters!*

A fabrication, of course, but it was the least I could do for Tanya Millhouse, whom I still cared about after all, but oddly enough, in more of a "brotherly" way than anything else. Her eyes lit up after I spoke, though. They lit up real good. Perhaps she was insulted by my aloof manner, or maybe just scarred by that image of Fred Hurley's wife showing up at McDonald's with her bible in one hand, and a baseball bat in the other. But whatever spooked Tanya, I'll never know...

Because just like that, I was thirty again!

A little sore over that all too brief "twenty again" moment, not having time to live through a few fantasies I had deftly put together in my mind after letting Tanya off the hook, I stood in the kitchen of my apartment. My apartment. My home. This was my home, the place where I've lived for over ten years now, yet things were somehow different.

Things were different in a manner that *Friends* was playing on my television, my old girlfriend Cynthia sat on my couch, and I had my hand on the door handle of my fridge, preparing to open it up and retrieve whatever it was I planned on retrieving (probably a beer), I can't remember, when all of a sudden, the phone rang...

Déjà vu materializes into cold hard fact. A cold hard fact with zero trace of *resemblance*. I knew what time it was then. I knew whose voice stood waiting inside that black box hung on my kitchen wall. I knew the words that waited there also, little bandits of emotion that they were, biding their time, tormenting their creator with anxiety while they held their poisoned daggers out for the ready. Ready for me.

Your father, Tom... his liver... well, the doctor says... um... well, you see, you might wanna come out here. Yeah, Tom... you might wanna come out here... really quick. Don't wait, Tom.

Don't wait? Don't wait, Tom?

Don't wait; so that bastard of an alcoholic ends up dying by himself? Don't let that emotional wreck, that abuser of the mind with his occasional head-spanking from the back of his hand just to sink things in—don't let this man go to his grave without so much as a goodbye from his only son? His only son, whom he hasn't heard from for ten years now, because ten years ago that boy finally broke his nose. Broke it damn good, for real-like, smashed and bloody after that old man went off on another one of his violent trips with the bottle, hitting and yelling, shattering windows and hearts with such nasty selfishness. *Slaying souls* with that nasty selfishness. A selfishness that could only be pounded, heated, folded, pounded, cooled, *forged,* honed... and then expertly swung by the clever hands of a drunk.

Don't let this man die alone... *again?*

***

Cynthia was a much nicer woman that I remembered her to be. A kinder woman, lovelier in all the ways she could be, while she sat there in the passenger seat of that car I drove to Riverside. The car I drove to that hospital in that same city, where on the seventh floor there was a particular room with a particular bed that contained the still warm body of a particularly cold man...

A cold man who waited.

But for the first time in my life... I saw him. I saw his eyes... His eyes... they were scared. They looked up at me, and although I've never had kids, and I don't really know the feelings parents have, but it was like... well... it was like my father, the old man that he was, all crumpled up under those covers of that hospital bed, with those eyes of his, I could've sworn...

And the coldness of this man, this soul, chilled no doubt from the incessant swallows of liquor... That coldness was gone. Vanquished by impending doom, and he really seemed *lost* because of it. Lost and alone, a scared little child. My child, perhaps.

And for the first time in my life, I reached out for this man. I reached out with my hand, a strong hand, a hand that told him—after he grabbed it so damn hard the way he did—told him I would never let him go.

And finally, for the first time in both of our lives, I heard the vibrant resonance of love in this man's voice. I heard all the pain, forever dampened by the gush of a million swigs. I heard it all come screaming out of him from those two simple words he spoke. Those two beautiful, life-altering words. Words that put to rest once and for all my decades of sorrow as they came whispering out of him.

My son.

And then, just like that, I heard the crashing of the waves.

Need something to read?
Go here:
Print: https://www.hiraethsffh.com/product-page/to-the-shore-to-the-sea-by-erica-ruppert
ePub: https://www.hiraethsffh.com/product-page/to-the-shore-to-the-sea-by-erica-ruppert-2
PDF: https://www.hiraethsffh.com/product-page/to-the-shore-to-the-sea-by-erica-ruppert-1

Who?

Lisa Timpf is a retired HR and communications professional who lives in Simcoe, Ontario. When not writing, Lisa enjoys organic gardening, bird watching, and taking long walks with her cocker spaniel-Jack Russell mix Chet. Lisa's speculative fiction has appeared in *NewMyths, Home for the Howlidays, Cosmic Crime*, and other venues. Lisa's collection of speculative haibun poetry, *In Days to Come*, is available from Hiraeth Publishing. You can find out more about Lisa's writing at http://lisatimpf.blogspot.com/.

Born in Cuba, **Matias Travieso-Diaz** migrated to the United States as a young man to escape political persecution. He became an engineer and lawyer and practiced for nearly fifty years. After retirement, he took up creative writing. Over eighty of his short stories have been published or accepted for publication in anthologies and paying magazines, blogs, audio books and podcasts. Some of his unpublished works have also received "honorable mentions" from several paying publications. A first collection of his stories, "The Satchel and Other Terrors" has recently been released and is available on Amazon and other book outlets.

Chris Riley lives near Sacramento, California, vowing one day to move back to the Pacific Northwest. In the meantime, he teaches special education, writes cool stories, and hides from the blasting heat for six months of the year. He has had over 100 short stories published in various magazines and anthologies, and across various genres. He is the author of the literary suspense novels *The Sinking of the Angie Piper* and *The Broken Pines.* For more information, go to www.chrisrileyauthor.com.

www.ingramcontent.com/pod-product-compliance
Lightning Source LLC
LaVergne TN
LVHW012035060526
838201LV00061B/4619